MW00777766

THE
STRONGEST
CORD

THE
STRONGEST
CORD

Brenda Minton

Five Star • Waterville, Maine

First Edition
First Printing: September 2006

Published in 2006 in conjunction with Tekno Books.

Set in 11 pt. Plantin.

Printed in the United States on permanent paper.

Library of Congress Cataloging-in-Publication Data

Minton, Brenda.
    The strongest cord / Brenda Minton.—1st ed.
      p. cm.
    ISBN 1-59414-492-3 (hc : alk. paper)
    1. Nurses—Fiction.   2. Children of prisoners—
Fiction.   3. Nieces—Fiction.   4. Cowboys—Fiction.
5. Oklahoma—Fiction.   I. Title.
PS3613.I69S77 2006
   813'.6—dc22   2006008409

Throughout this writing journey, and it has been a journey, there have been so many people who have supported me, believed in me, and put up with me. I want to thank them all, and I want to thank God for giving my life purpose.

Doug, Josh, Luke and Hannah, this one is for the four of you. You've put up with the dirty laundry, fast food, and ten years of waiting.

To my family, each and every one of you, for believing I could do this and for encouraging me to dream. Dad, Ellen, Janice, Mike, Keri, Aunt Bet . . . to all of you, the list is long.

To my friends, for not giving up on me. For reading, critiquing, and always being honest. Even when it hurt. The labor was long, but the baby has finally been delivered.

Stephanie, Angela, Dawn, Lori, Barbara and Cheryl . . . Where would I be without friends? Probably more insane than I already am.

To Janet, the agent who wouldn't give up. Thank you for putting up with me.

To Five Star for the opportunity, and for making this such a great experience.

To the readers, for reading. Thank you all.

CHAPTER 1

Ian Hunt wanted nothing more than to get home. He'd had a long night at work at the hospital, a night that hadn't produced a happy ending. Nights like that sucked the joy out of his day. He wondered how people got through without faith, without something to believe in.

Hot air, heavy with humidity, struck him full in the face as he walked out of the grocery store. It would feel good to sit down with a glass of iced tea, and maybe later spend time with a yearling colt he had bought the week before.

Working with his horses brought him a sense of calm. He needed that today. He needed time to be alone with God and to feel the peace that only He could bring.

A child's laughter, carefree as a summer day, blended with carousel music. He glanced in the direction of the purple mechanical horse at the front of the store. The child, a girl with blond curls and round cheeks, leaned forward over the stretched-out neck of the horse.

A smile sneaked up on him, chasing away the melancholia that had blanketed him for the last few hours. The little girl slapped the mechanical horse with the reins. Ian smiled, knowing that in her mind she was a jockey on a Kentucky Derby contender, or rounding the third barrel in the National Championship Rodeo Finals.

Her laughter helped him to forget how wrong last night had gone.

His gaze shifted from the little girl to the tall brunette standing nearby. The music, the child, and the heat of the day faded as his gaze locked on the woman and recognition hit him with the force of a semi truck. The sight of her took him back to his seventeenth summer and to those first feelings of puppy love. As if she felt his eyes on her, she turned.

Lilly Tanner had been gone for fourteen years. He'd had fourteen years of wondering how she had fared in life and if she had married or had children. He had hoped, wished, for the best for her, and prayed that she would return.

A woman with a cartload of groceries and two unhappy children pushed past him. He mumbled an apology for standing in her way and stepped to the side of the door. Lilly hadn't moved. Her gaze rested on him for a moment, and then darted nervously in the direction of the parking lot. Like a skittish deer, she seemed startled and about to escape.

What had sent her running home, to a place that had filled her childhood with pain and bad memories? Years ago he had put her on a bus heading north, her little sister in tow. She had thanked him and then said they would probably never see each other again.

Since it was obvious he wasn't her reason for returning, he moved on to more plausible reasons. He couldn't think of one, not when her last words to him had been something to the tune of, "Thank you. You're a good friend."

She looked away from him and reached for the little girl. The child shook her head and grabbed the reins, making it clear she wasn't finished riding the horse.

Ian dug into his pocket and pulled out a quarter. He crossed to where Lilly stood and dropped the coin into the box attached to the horse. The child froze, her happy smile disappearing at his nearness.

The reaction faded as music filled the air and the horse took off on another run through imaginary fields. He remembered doing the same thing as a child.

"You're back." He winced at the line. Of all the things he could have said, or asked, that seemed like the most inane. He could have said, "Hi, Lilly, I didn't know you were back.'" Or maybe, "Lilly, it's been a long time. How have you been?" Instead he uttered two words and managed to sound like an addled teenager. The half-grin on her face let him know what she thought of his statement.

He glanced at the little girl and then down to Lilly's ring finger. No diamond glinted there, not even a plain gold band.

"Hello to you, too, Ian. But can't you think of something better to say? You were always more original than that." Her voice still held that husky timbre that could turn a man into mush, and this time it mixed with a hint of laughter.

"Give me a minute to get over my shock." He reached for his hat, pushed it back and then forward again.

"Still playing cowboy?" The words were said with a smile, but he knew how she really felt. Or had felt.

"Yes, still playing."

The horse had stopped and the little girl sat still as a mouse about to be pounced on by a barn cat. Her big eyes were glued to him, to his hat, and then down to his boots. Fear mingled with curiosity as she raised her head and briefly made eye contact.

"Do you need help down, sweetie?" He reached, but didn't move forward.

"Are you a real cowboy?" She whispered the question, but declined his offer for help by sliding off the side of the horse and taking her place at Lilly's side.

Lilly shook her head and laughed. "No, Shelby, he's a wannabe."

The child squinted and studied his face as if she were

9

looking for signs of illness. Her gaze traveled away from him to Lilly. "What's a wannabe?"

Ian kneeled next to her and he pulled off his hat. "I'm a real cowboy, Shelby. Do you like horses?"

The child nodded, biting down on her lip as she stared at him. Ian moved back a foot, giving her space.

"If you ask Lilly, maybe you could stop by and see my horses."

Lilly shook her head at him. "Don't do this, Ian."

He winked at the child before standing back up to face Lilly. Always tall, with high heels she looked him in the eye, a direct gaze, as warm as the summer sun, but hidden behind a cloud.

"Don't do what, Lilly? We were friends; there's no reason to act like strangers, or enemies."

She looked down, her fingers stroking through the blond ringlets of the child who held on to the hem of her shirt with clenched fingers.

"You're right, Ian, we're not enemies. You were definitely a friend."

"So, as a friend, if you need anything, you know that I'm here."

"I know that you're here. But honest, I don't need anything."

He somehow doubted that. It would take more than a common case of homesickness to bring her back to Oklahoma. The troubled look in her eyes, and the fear reflected in the face of the child at her side told more than words.

"Okay, but the offer stands." And he knew to leave it at that.

"The only thing I really need is a job."

She had achieved her goal of graduating from nursing

school. He had loaned her the money to relocate and when she paid it back, she had let him know about her new life, and her degree. The thing she had failed to do was include a return address. That hadn't been a mistake. She hadn't wanted to be found.

"I could help. I know people at the hospital." The doubt in her eyes wouldn't let him tell her more than that. She had never trusted cowboys. Shoot, just wearing a pair of boots was a crime in her mind.

"Thank you, Ian. I really do appreciate that." Cool, polite, her tone put him in the place of forgotten acquaintance, and not the friend he had once been.

He glanced down at his dusty Ropers and noticed that she wore sandals. Her toes were painted red and matched the shirt she wore with her white capri pants. The gangly girl, part she-cat and part Cherokee, who used to walk barefoot down dirt roads, was gone.

He had a feeling he would miss her if he couldn't find her inside this more polished version of that girl. He doubted he could get this version to sneak into the feedlot down the road and ride hogs until the farmer chased them off. And he probably couldn't talk her into skipping school and going to the lake.

He had always enjoyed pulling Lilly into mischief. She had enjoyed it, too, when she hadn't been thinking about how wrong it was, or about the things she should have been doing.

"Good-bye, Ian."

She reached for the little girl's hand. If the child wasn't Lilly's, then whose was she? Where were her parents, and what did this have to do with Lilly coming home? And why did both Lilly and Shelby have twin looks of apprehension lurking in their eyes? Questions rumbled through his mind, as the two looked to be about to escape.

"Aunt Lilly, can we still get a hamburger?" *Aunt*—that solved that mystery. The little girl had to belong to Missy, Lilly's younger sister.

"Yes, honey, we can get a hamburger." She picked up the child and placed her in the seat of the nearby grocery cart.

Ian dropped his groceries into the cart next to Lilly's, avoiding the look she shot him. He reached for the cart's handle, effectively taking control of the situation, and obviously pushing Lilly a little further in the direction of impatience.

Shelby's teeth were implanted in her bottom lip as she stared up at him with a mixture of fear and awe. He sought to ease her mind, somehow, some way. He winked and smiled, drawing a small grin in return.

A bigger smile took its place when he pulled off his cowboy hat and placed it on her head. It slid down over her eyes and she pushed it back with a pudgy hand.

"I can manage my own groceries." Lilly walked next to him.

"I'm sure you can, Lil. You've always managed." He pushed the cart of what appeared to be mostly snack foods away from the building and out of the shade.

Waves of heat rolled up from the blacktop. It felt more like July than late September. Ian wiped his arm across his brow and then smiled down at the child who still stared up at him. He winked and she smiled again, this time without the fear that had lurked behind her eyes.

Too bad Lilly couldn't be as easily won over. Cowboys didn't impress Lilly Tanner. She had her reasons, good reasons, but it sure made it hard for a guy in boots to impress her.

"Where's your car?"

"The van, over there." She pointed to a newer minivan. He never would have guessed it to be hers. What happened to her dreams of a red convertible?

"Where are you staying?" he asked as she unlocked the side door.

"For now we're staying at a hotel in town."

"At a hotel?"

"Yes, at a hotel."

Ian grabbed her groceries and started stowing them behind the last row of seats. She stood next to him, arms crossed in front of her, and a troubled look in her dark, doe eyes. She gave independence a whole new meaning.

"There, all done." He reached into his pocket and pulled out a couple of tickets. "There's a rodeo tonight. Why don't you bring Shelby? She might see some real cowboys."

Lilly actually smiled at that. She even chuckled a little. Not much, but enough to chase away the worry from her eyes, and to show him that the real Lilly was in there somewhere. The thaw only lasted a moment, but long enough to give him hope.

"Could we, Aunt Lilly?" Shelby had those big eyes zeroed in on her aunt. Ian didn't see any way for Lilly to turn her down.

"I don't know, Shelby. We'll think about it."

Ian smiled at the child. "See you, kiddo."

"Ian . . ."

He turned, expecting a lecture. Instead she looked pensive, like she might need to talk. She shrugged, and then shook her head.

"Never mind."

"What is it, Lilly? Can I help?"

He reached for Shelby. The little girl hesitated but then lifted her arms for him to pick her up. As soon as he set her

13

down she climbed into the van, and the safety of her booster seat.

Lilly buckled the little girl in, and closed the van door before turning. She looked down, focusing on a red blob of gum near her foot, her hands shoved into her pockets.

"I need to go." She kept her head turned away from him.

"If you need me, you know where to find me. I'm still at Grandad's farm."

She nodded and he let her escape. Sometimes he knew when to quit pushing. This happened to be one of those times.

Lilly sat behind the wheel of the van for a few minutes, and prayed that coming home had really been God's will. She could have stayed in Kansas City, or picked one of a dozen other locations. But for some reason she had felt this was God's answer to her prayers.

She had hoped they could be safe here, and that Shelby's father, Carl Long, wouldn't be able to find them. Since Lilly had been given custody of her niece, she had felt as if her whole life had been turned upside down and flipped over backwards.

Everything had changed. She had suddenly been thrown into the role of mother to a child she had seen only once every few months or so—usually when Missy had needed something. She had given up her job and her apartment to find a new life. For a person who liked things to be in order, this felt like anything but.

She hadn't felt safe for weeks. She couldn't begin to imagine how her niece felt.

What Lilly didn't need was Ian Hunt in her life, adding to the upheaval. Old habits that she had thought were gone, buried with her past, were lurking, trying to come out of hiding. As much as she wanted to take care of herself, it would be too easy to turn to Ian. He knew how to solve problems, and she had a big one.

Ian should have been gone. Or so she had told herself when she drove back into town. He would have had his fill of playing cowboy, and he would have gone back to his home in Boston, back to his life of ease. Ian had been a fish out of water in Oklahoma. He had been a good-hearted kid who had wanted a few years of country life on his grandfather's ranch.

He was just a thorn. Okay, not a thorn. He was . . . he was . . . she couldn't think what to call him.

"Was that man a friend, Aunt Lilly? 'Cause we don't talk to strangers, do we?" The voice came from the backseat, helping her to make sense of her thoughts, and bringing a smile she hadn't counted on.

"Yes, Shelby, a long time ago he was a friend."

He had been the person she'd turned to when she needed help. And he had always helped.

He was also the person she most often pushed away. Ian managed to get under her skin faster than anyone else.

And because of Ian, she was a nurse. She couldn't forget that. She had a life that she enjoyed. She had managed to follow her dreams, and to make them come true.

All because of Ian. No strings attached, he had said, when he wrote her a check that she insisted had to be a loan. Strings are funny things; even when not implied, they exist.

"Aunt Lilly, I'm hungry."

Lilly glanced in the rearview mirror. She smiled at her niece, who had her thumb in her mouth and a stuffed animal hugged to her chin. The thumb sucking had become a real problem in the last few months. Lilly just didn't have the heart to make her stop. For now the child seemed to need the comfort of the habit.

The reason for the thumb sucking could be hiding any-where, waiting to take Shelby, or worse. Lilly touched the button on the door panel, locking them inside the safety of the van as she checked the mirrors, praying she wouldn't see lurking figures waiting to follow them.

"I'm really, really hungry."

Lilly glanced over her shoulder, and managed a quick smile for her niece.

"Okay, hamburgers it is." She shifted into reverse and backed out of the parking place. A few spaces over she saw Ian getting into a big red truck.

For the longest time she had convinced herself that Oklahoma was the place of hard times and bad memories. Funny how seeing him had stirred up all of the good memo-ries of this place and her life here.

"You're not going to believe who's home." Ian poured himself a glass of juice and pushed the refrigerator door shut with his foot.

Kathy, his housekeeper, cook, and on-site mother figure, stopped cooking and turned to give him a quizzical look. She disliked guessing games, and he knew it. She had told him that more than once. Now she said it with a look. More ap-propriately . . . *the look*. The one that turned down one side of her mouth and at the same time drew her eyebrows together.

That same look used to send him running for cover. But that had been fifteen—no, maybe two—years ago. He had grown up a lot since then. He no longer feared his house-keeper. Most of the time.

Even her husband Johnny knew enough to keep a healthy, fearful respect for the woman that kept their lives running and in order.

She fed them, cleaned for them, kept them organized. And when they needed it, she put them back on the straight and narrow.

"You know I'm not going to guess." She turned her attention back to the stir-fry.

Ian grinned and leaned against the counter. "You'll never guess in a million years," he teased.

"I don't plan on trying, so you might as well tell me." The corner of her mouth now lifted in a telltale smile. She was curious. He knew her so well.

"Someone very special to us both."

"Pastor Barker? I thought he was still in Mexico." She sprinkled soy sauce over the chicken and vegetable mixture. Ian inhaled the aroma of the chicken and garlic. His stomach rumbled in response.

"Not even close."

"I told you, I don't want to play this game." She turned off the burner under the pan. "And if you don't tell me, I'll just toss this out to the dog."

"We don't have a dog."

"Ian." Her warning tone matched the look.

"Okay, I'll tell you, but you won't believe it. Lilly is in town. And she has a child with her, a little girl with blond hair. She looks like Missy."

"Well, I declare." Kathy touched her fingers to her temples. "Did you tell her to come out and see me?"

"I haven't really had a chance. I've talked to her, but she doesn't seem very happy to see me. To be honest, she seems a little nervous."

"Don't push her, Ian. You know she needs space." She put a lid over the rice before continuing. "You know how she feels about this place. The memories here are too much for her. She wouldn't come back unless there was a reason."

Ian knew that as well as anyone, and he doubted if he counted as a good enough reason to come home. "I think I've given her space." He emptied the contents of his glass and stuck it in the dishwasher. "I bought her the bus ticket, and I've given her fourteen years of space."

"You were a good friend to her." Kathy patted his cheek. "And she's sure to remember that."

A good friend. Exactly what every guy wants to be.

"Can we go to the rodeo, Aunt Lilly?"

Lilly turned away from the hotel sink and tried to smile. She wanted to say no. But she couldn't, not when it meant so much to her niece. Shelby needed some fun times. She needed memories that would produce something other than nightmares. Going to a rodeo was something she had wanted for so long.

A normal Friday evening with other families out for a good time, eating hot dogs from the concession stand smothered in ketchup and relish. What would it hurt? And wasn't that the reason, or one of the reasons, Lilly had brought Shelby to Oklahoma—for a fresh start, and a chance at a normal life?

And to hide from Carl, Shelby's father.

Visions of Missy's spiral into the world of drug addiction resurfaced in Lilly's mind. She closed her eyes to force the memory away. She had tried so hard to be a parent to her sister. She had failed. Missy had needed more than a sister only a few years her senior could give.

Another image took over, the violent face of Shelby's father when he vowed to find his daughter and get her back. The next day he had escaped from the police as they transferred him to the county facility.

Lilly wouldn't let him hurt her niece. She had custody,

and Shelby would never suffer the way Lilly and her sister had suffered.

This time Lilly wouldn't fail to protect her loved ones. She would protect Shelby the way she hadn't been able to protect Missy.

"Aunt Lilly, are you okay?"

She opened her eyes and managed a smile. "Yes, sweet, I'm fine. And yes, we can go to the rodeo. You need to get out of that bed and get your shoes on."

Shelby jumped out of the bed where she'd been sleeping for the last two hours. Instead of getting her shoes, the little girl ran to Lilly and wrapped pudgy four-year-old arms around her waist.

Lilly sucked in a deep breath at the rush of emotion that enveloped her as those little arms squeezed her middle. For months Shelby had been so silent, so stoic, and so frightened. Seeing her niece smile again made coming back to Oklahoma worth it all.

"I love you, Aunt Lilly."

"I love you, too."

She loved her niece enough to put her own heart in danger. Ian would be at that rodeo and she knew him well enough to know that he would push until she opened up, exposing her fears. And that would make her vulnerable to other emotions. The ones she'd been fighting since the day seventeen-year-old Ian Hunt arrived at his grandfather's farm.

He had been full of laughter and lighthearted fun, never taking life seriously. She had been almost fifteen and trying to hold her family together with parents who had never seemed to grow up.

Memories of Ian shouldn't bother her. Memories shouldn't accompany country songs that reminisced about teenage years and county fairs. Those songs were too close to the real thing.

"Aunt Lilly, you're staring at the wall again."

Lilly laughed and shook her head. "Yes, I guess I am. I'm sorry, sweetheart. Let me get my hair dry and we'll go."

The rodeo grounds were already packed when Lilly and Shelby arrived. A volunteer on a black-and-white paint horse motioned for them to park at the end of the row. Shelby eased her van through the grass field that served as a parking lot to a space at the end.

"We're here, we're here." Shelby was already unbuckling her seatbelt and climbing out of her seat, showing more animation than she had in weeks.

Adjusting to one another had taken time. Being thrown together permanently after only having had sporadic visits had taken some getting used to. Overcoming the loss of Missy had hurt them both. It didn't help, knowing that in a few years they would get her back. They missed her now.

"Yes, we're here." Lilly tried taking a deep breath, but the rolling of her stomach didn't lessen. Motion sickness without the motion.

Ian sickness.

He always did this to her, maybe because he had always seemed to be in constant motion and he had dragged her along in the craziness of his life.

"Come on, Lil, have fun, loosen up," he would say. How odd. She still couldn't see anything fun about jumping on the back of Farmer Dalton's feeder hogs and riding them through the muck and mud.

She chuckled to herself anyway. Especially as the memory kicked into gear, bringing back the way they had slipped and slid as they ran through the mud holding hands.

Let go of the past, she told herself as she stepped out of her van. *Don't let Ian Hunt be your white knight. Especially don't rely on a cowboy.*

She had learned the lesson from her mother: *Cowboys will tell you what you want to hear and then they'll break your heart. They'll keep breaking it until it shatters. Go somewhere, Lilly. Have an adventure, but don't think a cowboy is going to make your dreams come true.*

Shelby tugged at her hand and Lilly looked down, into the smiling face of her niece. The little girl had insisted on wearing her red boots, jeans, western shirt, and a white hat—clothes that Missy had bought for her.

Lilly's younger sister had wanted nothing more than to be a cowgirl herself. And look where those dreams had gotten her. Lilly choked on guilt and regret. Maybe if she had stayed, rather than dragging fifteen-year-old Missy off to Kansas City, away from the farm life that the younger girl had loved, things would have been better.

Maybe, or maybe not. A sermon her pastor had preached returned to her mind. She couldn't live in the past, tangled up in what ifs.

It took work, untangling herself from that web of what ifs.

Now Shelby looked like every little girl's idea of a cowgirl. Horses, ranches, rodeos: it all seemed like some romantic fairy tale to a child who didn't know about unpaid bills, hunger, and watching a little sister cry herself to sleep while her own stomach rumbled.

Not that Shelby's childhood had been easy. For one so young, she'd seen her own share of problems. But Shelby had an aunt who now had the ability to keep their lives in order.

Chaos was something Lilly couldn't handle. She liked everything neat and orderly, in the proverbial box—so to speak.

Shelby tugged on her hand again, reminding her that she'd been lost in her thoughts. She smiled, and gave the tiny hand a gentle squeeze.

"Ready to go, kiddo?"

"Yes, yes." Shelby jerked her toward the arena.

After buying hot dogs, nachos and colas they found a seat on the bottom row of the bleachers, close to the dust of the arena. Shelby was thrilled with the close proximity. Lilly would rather have found a place elsewhere, far from the dust, the noise, and the action—like back at the hotel. She plastered a smile on her face for her niece's benefit.

The rodeo started and they settled in with their food, eating and cheering with the crowd. Shelby held a toy lariat that they'd bought at the concession stand. Every now and then she would sling it in a circle around her head and let it land on Lilly, who mooed and did a horrible job at being a lassoed calf.

"Where is Ian?" Shelby, with a mouth full of chips, asked the question an hour after their arrival.

"Swallow your food." Lilly glanced in the direction of the chutes and holding pens. "There he is."

He saw them and raised his hat in greeting. Lilly sucked in her breath and questioned her sanity.

"Isn't he going to ride?" Shelby sounded disappointed.

"I'm not sure, Shelby."

So far they had seen the saddle bronc, the calf roping and barrel racing competition. Of course he hadn't really said he participated. Maybe he just helped.

Bull riding was announced. Lilly held her breath, almost fearing the announcement. She could leave; she didn't have to watch. Her heart raced and her mind whirled back to her seventeenth summer.

A late night, a knock on the door, the fallen face of her mother as a police officer and stock contractor from the rodeo broke the news of her father's death.

He had died the way he lived, trying to cheat the odds. That last time the bull won, and her father lost.

"There he is." Shelby's happy squeal yanked Lilly back into the present. "He is a real cowboy, Aunt Lilly."

Lilly's gaze went to the front of the arena just as the announcer said Ian's name and gave the name of the bull that had never been ridden for eight seconds. Wonderful. He was going to get killed right in front of them—and in less than eight seconds.

CHAPTER 2

Lilly reached for Shelby's hand.

"Let's go. We don't need to watch this."

Shelby, normally a compliant child, didn't budge. "But I wanna watch."

Lilly tried to argue, but Shelby, always obedient—sometimes too obedient—wouldn't budge. The rodeo had drawn the child momentarily from the quiet shell she had ducked into when her mother had been arrested.

"Shelby, this isn't something we want to watch."

Too late. The gate opened and the bull came spinning from the chute. The beast shook his big head, throwing foamy saliva in all directions. Ian moved with the twisting gyrations of the animal as it turned in circles, bucking, trying to free itself from the man on its back. The roar of the crowds blended with the snorting of the animal.

Lilly sat frozen on the metal bench, clenching her fingers around the edge of the seat. She wanted to close her eyes but couldn't. Next to her Shelby screamed Ian's name. The bull came up off the ground, all four feet in the air. It twisted in midair and landed with a thud that shook its rider like a rag doll.

Unable to watch, Lilly closed her eyes.

"Don't let him die." She heard herself say the words, and knew that it was a prayer.

The buzzer rang, signaling the end of the ride. Lilly opened one eye a crack and saw him still on the bull's back, not on the ground, trampled under its deadly hooves. He'd made it: the first man to ride Tulsa Twister. The crowd went wild. Shelby stood on the bleacher, clapping and screaming.

Lilly's gaze remained glued to the man on the bull. She watched as he struggled to release his hand. The bull twisted and Ian went off, landing on his feet. The bull jerked around, knocking him into the air.

Shelby stopped clapping and leaned against Lilly's shoulder. The two of them watched in horror as the bullfighters in their bright clown makeup tried to distract the animal.

Ian slid to the ground and a hushed silence fell over the arena. The crowds of people sat on the edges of their seats. The announcer whispered a quiet suggestion that the folks say a prayer for the cowboy. Lilly heard a few murmured words from the people around her. She watched as a couple of cowboys kneeled next to Ian's prone body, hats in their hands as they prayed.

Shelby sobbed, and Lilly drew her close. As she watched Ian, motionless on the ground, she fought with opposing emotions: fear and anger. Anger because he'd managed to get her here and then he let this happen. Fear because she didn't want him to die.

She still needed to tell him thank you for what he'd done for her. He deserved more than a note in a card and a check.

A paramedic ran to the fallen man who was now trying to sit up. He was alive, giving her first dibs at killing him. She brushed at a few tears that had managed to squeeze out of her eyes. Angry tears, she told herself.

He held his arm as the men helped him to his feet. The crowd cheered and Ian limped out of the dusty arena.

"Let's go, Shelby."

"Back to the hotel?"

Lilly stood up, gripping her niece's hand a little too tightly. "No, we'll check on the stupid fool first."

"Fool isn't a nice word, Aunt Lilly." She squinted at the ground. "And I don't think stupid is, either."

No, it wasn't. They weren't. She nodded in agreement and led her niece toward the back of the arena. Even from a distance she could see the ambulance and the crowd gathered around it.

As they neared the back of the red vehicle, she saw Ian. He looked up from his seat on the stretcher and gave her a half-grin followed by a wince, rather than the customary wink. The paramedic standing in front of him tightened a sling around his neck and then helped him down from the back of the vehicle. The arm obviously wasn't broken. Irrationality being her strongest emotion at the moment, she considered breaking it for him.

"You sure you don't want to go in and have that examined?" the paramedic asked.

"I'm sure." Ian smiled her way again.

"Well, you're the . . ."

"The guy with a wrenched shoulder that will be fine in a few days." Ian finished the other man's sentence and then headed her way.

"You'll never grow up," were the words she picked. Those words seemed safest—much safer than, "I don't want you to die." Or even, "Please don't do that again."

Fourteen years and he was still twisting her insides. She still couldn't be composed in his presence.

Ian was a synonym for chaos.

"I don't plan on it." He answered her insult about growing up and, reaching down with his good hand, plucked at Shelby's blond curls. "Hey, cowgirl."

"You really are a cowboy." The child's eyes grew wide

with admiration. Lilly groaned. Of all the men for her niece to pick as a role model. She tried to push aside those feelings and concentrate instead on the fact that Shelby wasn't afraid of Ian. That was a good thing. Even she had to admit that.

"Something like it," Ian answered.

He turned to smile at Lilly and she wanted to smack him. She really disliked him at that moment. Not only did he go and get hurt on her first night back in town, but he looked too stinking good. Tall and rugged with too-long brown hair streaked blond from the sun, and those hazel eyes that always seemed to be dancing with laughter.

She tried to find something wrong with him, just to make herself feel better. He was dusty, dirty, and his hair was too long. There, that felt better.

"Are you mad at me, Lil?" When had he lost his East Coast accent and perfected that Oklahoma drawl?

"You better believe I am." She glared, to prove her point. But that glare descended, taking in his torn, faded jeans and those cute knees of his peeking through the holes.

"Can you give me a lift home?" He grinned, exposing that one maddening dimple in his right cheek. "I took some painkillers and I'm afraid they're starting to kick in. I'm seeing two of you, and you're both mad."

Lilly sighed. "Yes, I can give you a ride."

She wasn't as mad as she wanted to be.

The painkillers took effect quicker than Ian thought they would. His eyes were growing heavy as the van drove away from the rodeo grounds. The pain in his shoulder lessened and his mind grew fuzzy.

"Hey, don't you go to sleep." Lilly's voice came from far away, pulling him back to his surroundings.

"You know where I live," he mumbled.

"Yes, I know where you live. But I don't plan on carrying you inside." She turned onto the main road and headed in the direction that would take them away from town. "I like what you've done with the place."

"The old farm burned down about five years ago. Gramps died six months later." He didn't expand on that. He might have, but he couldn't get his mouth to cooperate.

"I'm sorry, I didn't know."

"You've been gone a long time. How could you have known?" His eyes closed, opening again as the van came to a stop.

"Ian, wake up." Her voice shook him, or maybe it was her hand on his arm. He moved away from the pain and tried to force his eyes open.

"I'm awake." Even to his ears the words sounded muffled, as if he had a mouth full of cotton.

He shook his head to clear the fog. The movement jarred his shoulder, sending a white-hot flash of pain down his arm. He closed his eyes, and gripped his left elbow with his right hand. He was really getting too old for this.

"Do you have to lecture me?" His eyes tried to close again. He should have waited to take those pills.

"I didn't say a word. You were talking to yourself." Laughter crept into her tone. "You really are a case."

Silence followed, and his eyes closed again.

Cool night air washed over his face a moment later. Or at least he assumed it was a moment. He opened his eyes to see Lilly standing in the open door, a puzzled look on her face. He reached up and touched her cheek.

"You're still beautiful." He managed to get the words out in almost intelligible English.

"You're still too sure of yourself." She shook her head

28

and leaned into the van, drawing closer and bringing the scent of something light and floral.

Ian turned as she put an arm around his good shoulder to draw him out of the van. He moved his feet out of the van and onto the paved driveway. Unfortunately, his legs didn't really feel like working. Falling slightly forward like an old man on a seven-day drunk, he stumbled against Lilly. She wrapped her arms around his waist to steady him.

Somehow his nose came into contact with her hair. *Good thinking, nose.* He nuzzled against her and inhaled the herbal scent of her shampoo. His lips managed to graze her neck before she pushed him away.

"You smell good." He smiled and a look of annoyance flashed across her face.

"Either you start walking, Ian, or I'm leaving you out here on the grass."

Ian got the picture. He turned toward the porch and her arm tightened around his waist. As they made their way to the front door, he honestly tried to keep his bearings to make it easier for her to help him.

"You could stay here." He dug into his pocket for his house keys. "You could marry me and live here forever."

She didn't respond, but he thought he saw her smile. Not that he could tell with his eyes crossing the way they were.

The key slipped into the lock and the door opened. He had the pleasure of hearing her gasp as she stepped into his home.

"Do you like it?"

She shrugged, "It's nice."

"I have plenty of room."

She ignored him.

"I'll get you to the couch and then you're on your own."

She helped him cross the expanse of hardwood floors to the leather sofa.

She eased him down and he leaned back on a throw pillow, glad for the support, even though he felt like he was still falling. He squinted, focusing on her face as she hovered over him.

"Thank you," he mumbled, ready to let the pain medication take over. But he couldn't, not yet. He had to know that she was going to be okay. The troubled look in her eyes told him more than she was willing to say about her return to Oklahoma.

"Stay and let me help you." He moved his mouth and hoped that the words came out the way he intended.

"How can you help me? You can't even move."

"I can help. Tomorrow." He tried for a grin that didn't feel quite right.

"Of course you will, tomorrow." She backed away from him, her frown wavering. "This is exactly why I didn't want to go to the rodeo."

"Lilly, I can help." He rubbed at his face, wishing again that he hadn't taken those pain pills. He should have just toughed it out. "Tell me what I can do to help you."

She sighed and sat down near his feet. He felt her hands on his boots and relaxed as she pulled off one and then the other, letting them drop with twin thuds on the floor next to the sofa. The soft weight of a quilt dropped over him and he opened his eyes.

"I have plenty of room. Don't drag her back to the hotel this late at night. It's not as if I'm going to bother you."

He saw that she was considering his offer. "Lilly, you're safe with me, I've never . . ." Good grief, what did he almost tell her? The pills, he really shouldn't have taken them.

"You've never what, Ian?" Her face was close to his; he could feel her breath on his cheek. He kept his eyes closed, knowing he couldn't answer that question. Not tonight when he wasn't able to explain.

"What, Lilly? I don't know." He opened one eye a crack. "Stay here tonight. Kathy and Johnny live here. We won't be alone."

"You've never what?"

"Never."

He felt her hand, cool and gentle, touch his cheek and then move through his hair. He couldn't convince his eyes to open.

"You're a mess, Ian." She leaned forward and her lips touched his forehead in a feathery light kiss. He felt the shift of weight on the couch as she moved away from him. As he drifted further into a drug-induced sleep he heard the front door close.

Lilly walked out the front door, knowing that she had to go back to her hotel. Even with Kathy and Johnny living here, she couldn't stay. Ian would take over her life. She couldn't let him do that.

Not only would he take over, but he would bring chaos to the orderly existence she had created for herself. Okay, she could admit it hadn't been too orderly of late. But she had to hold on to some sense of normality. What used to be her life had become anything but, and she needed to find a way to reclaim what she had lost.

The dark night closed in on her and she shivered as a sliver of cold, unexplainable fear slid up her back, almost a physical touch. Somewhere in the distance a car engine roared to life. She tried to tell herself that it wasn't Carl, couldn't be him. He wouldn't know how to find her here.

Headlights flashed, cutting a path of light through the night sky. Just a neighbor coming home, she told herself. Or someone lost.

Or Carl.

Lilly pushed away the voice that told her to be strong, to take care of Shelby on her own. The old adage of doing it herself just didn't ring true. Not tonight. Not in the dark and with Carl out there somewhere.

She hurried to lift Shelby out of the van. With her arms full, she couldn't slide the door closed. She would come back later and close it. She glanced up and down the dark country road and shivered. Or maybe she wouldn't. If she left it open, what would it hurt? At least they would be safely inside, behind locked doors, and with people she knew.

She made it into the house, fumbled with the doorknob and then slowly made her way up the wide staircase. In the dark she groped along the wall, searching for a light switch. She finally found one. A low-wattage bulb came on in a carriage-type light that hung on the wall at the top of the stairs.

Her eyes adjusted and she surveyed her surroundings. Ian had done well for himself. Of course he had; with a trust fund and this farm, how could he have done poorly for himself?

The house wasn't ostentatious, but comfortable and decorated tastefully. The wide hall had wood floors like the downstairs. A narrow rug ran the full length, in deep earthy tones that blended with the wood.

There were four doors off the hall. She picked the first one, but quickly shut the door on a room that looked too personal, and too much like the owner of the house, with Native American artwork, a hand-sewn quilt on the bed, and a pair of shoes next to the door.

32

"We'll try the other side of the hall," she whispered to the child sleeping in her arms. She picked the far room, knowing the sun would rise on that side of the house and, if there were windows facing east, she would have a wonderful view of the field.

She turned the knob and pushed the door open with her shoulder. The room she stepped into was perfect, with a king-sized sleigh bed covered with a down comforter. Shelby woke up briefly when she put her down on the big bed. Her eyes fluttered and she smiled. Lilly kissed her brow and smoothed back the blond ringlets of hair.

"Go to sleep, sweetheart."

"I need Teddy and I need my nightie."

"We don't have them here, Shelby. But we'll go back to the hotel tomorrow."

"Where are we?"

Lilly sat down on the edge of the bed. "We're at Ian's ranch. He's hurt, remember? We're going to stay here to-night, and make sure he's okay."

And for this night they would be safe. She didn't tell Shelby about her fears, or about the danger they were in. Instead she kissed her on the forehead and told her to go back to sleep.

"Is he alive?" Ian felt a small hand on his face and the cushion of the sofa moved. "I think he might be dead. He's been sleeping a long time."

The little hand touched his chest as if she was feeling to see if his heart was beating. He kept his eyes closed and hid the smile that tried to slide on to his lips.

"He isn't dead, sweetie, but he'll wish he was when he wakes up. He'll probably be mean as an old bear after that fall and then sleeping on the couch."

Ian groaned and wished Kathy would be quiet. The lady was a gem and closer to him than his own mother. She was also more opinionated and bossy.

A little hand touched his and he opened his eyes enough to see Shelby's concerned look. While her attention was elsewhere, he worked up a good bear growl and reached to grab her with his good arm.

Shelby screeched and Kathy came running from the kitchen, a spatula in her hand. When she saw him she raised the stainless steel weapon and shook it. Her mouth twisted into a frown as she brandished the cooking utensil.

"Don't you scare that child," she warned.

Shelby burst into a fit of giggling and then a real belly laugh. Ian raised one brow and gave his cook/housekeeper an "I told you so" look.

When it came to kids, he did know a thing or two.

"Where's your Aunt Lilly?" he asked the little girl when she paused to catch her breath.

"She had to go to the hotel to get us some clean clothes. Kathy's making chocolate chip pancakes." All in one breath; he was impressed.

"And Kathy knows that isn't a healthy breakfast for a growing girl."

Kathy stepped back into the room, wiping flour-dusted hands on her apron. "And you can keep that expert opinion to yourself. If you complain, then I'll make you eat a boiled egg."

"I'm not complaining."

The housekeeper walked farther into the room. She shook her head at him, as if he was still seventeen.

"Last night could have been bad."

"Could have been, but it wasn't." He lifted his hand and tousled Shelby's blond curls. When had the child lost her fear? "I'm fine, Kathy."

She mumbled something as she walked away and he didn't ask her to repeat it. He didn't need to know what she thought about his bull riding. Besides that, he was almost ready to agree. He couldn't keep this up. His body wasn't getting any younger, and he didn't want to jeopardize his career.

"Can you get up?" Shelby asked, managing to sound a lot like Lilly. Her arms were crossed, her tiny chin raised a notch, and she gave him a speculative look.

"Sure I can, sweetie." The words were easier than the actual proving of them.

As Shelby watched, he managed to sit up. His shoulder screamed in protest and his whole body felt stiff—sort of like he'd been run over by a bull. At that moment he felt more like sixty than thirty-four.

"So, you're up and moving." Lilly stepped through the front door and made her way across the living room. It took him by surprise, having her walk into his house that way, as if it hadn't been years since she'd walked through his front door.

"I'm up. I don't know about moving." He let his gaze slide over the woman standing in front of him. Tall and not reed-thin, more majestic than dainty, she was no longer the barefoot girl of their teenage years.

He looked up and caught her watching him. Her face had always intrigued him. Not a beauty queen face, but a strong, beautiful face, with large eyes and a straight nose. Her mouth was wide and generous, but didn't smile nearly often enough.

"Stop staring, Ian."

"I'm sorry, just trying to adjust to seeing you like this," he explained.

Kathy interrupted by stepping out of the kitchen again.

He figured she did it on purpose, to defuse the situation or to keep him from saying something he would regret.

"Breakfast is almost ready and you're not eating until you've had a shower." She pointed the spatula at him. "I put clean clothes in the spare bedroom for you. I would recommend you get cleaned up, because even from here you smell like the arena—and it isn't pleasant."

Good thing he had the self-esteem thing covered at his age.

"Yes, ma'am." He took a deep breath and stood up, wobbling a little as he made it to his feet.

Lilly's hand came out, reaching for his arm. "You okay?"

"I'm fine." He took a step away from her to prove his point. "See, right as rain."

"Yes, you're fine." She snorted. "When you get out of the shower, I'll help you get that sling back on."

She didn't look as convinced when he walked out of the bathroom carrying his shirt and the sling. He held them out to her and watched as her gaze landed on the shirt.

"I can't get the shirt on."

She took it from him. With her bottom lip between her teeth, she held it out. Ian slipped his left arm in first, grimacing as he raised it to put his hand through the sleeve. Lilly stopped and moved around to look at him. He managed to shrug his right shoulder and smile.

"You need to go to the emergency room." She buttoned his shirt with fingers that fumbled. He held out the sling but didn't respond to her ER comment. She adjusted the sling and then tightened it around his neck.

"Try not to mistake that thing for a noose."

"Don't give me any ideas." She finished with the buckle. "There, that should do you until you get it checked out."

"I'm not going to get it checked out." He walked away

from her. She followed, taking the seat next to his at the dining room table.

"I really think . . ."

"I'm fine."

She snorted again. Shelby looked from him to her aunt and her bottom lip trembled. He smiled at the little girl and refrained from further comments. Whatever was going on with Lilly had obviously affected the child, and she didn't need the added trauma of seeing the two of them fighting.

"Chocolate chip pancakes," Kathy called out as she moved toward the table with a steaming plate of pancakes. "For lunch, I guess."

Ian looked at his watch and groaned. It was after eleven.

The telephone rang as he took his first bite of pancake. He watched Kathy hurry to answer it and he waited. She nodded and then handed it to him.

"I've got to go to work," he explained as he ended the call.

"You're going to work, like that?" Lilly put down her fork. "I don't know if that's a good idea."

He almost laughed. "I don't really have a choice. It's my department and I have to cover for someone who couldn't make it in."

"Your department?"

He should have known she wouldn't let it go. Glancing toward the kitchen, he saw Kathy give him an amused look. He turned his attention back to Lilly.

"Yes, at the hospital."

"What do you do there?" she asked.

"A little of everything," he hedged, not quite ready to tell her. He wouldn't lie to her, but he wasn't sure if she was ready to hear the whole story of his life.

How could he tell her, when she'd spent their teen years

thinking he planned to spend his life goofing off? In her mind he was just another wannabe cowboy, and she didn't like cowboys. Not that he blamed her. If he'd been in her shoes, he might have hated cowboys, too.

The cowboys in his life had all been heroes. His grandfather first, and then Johnny. Her father had been a different breed of cowboy, not the noble kind who rescued women and stray puppies.

"Ian?" She accepted a cup of coffee from Kathy with a smile of thank you and then shifted her serious brown eyes back in his direction. "I'm sure you have to go, but . . ."

"Gotta eat and run." He took a big bite of pancake.

Kathy snorted and he shot her a look that silenced any comment she might make. She headed back to the kitchen with the coffee pot, but he could hear her muttering at him.

How had he suddenly become outnumbered? It seemed that he was no longer the king of his castle, and he felt pretty sure he didn't like that idea.

"What time will you be back?" Lilly continued with her questions, following him to the living room when they finished breakfast.

Ian sat down on the couch and reached for his boots. The first one slid on easily. The second took more effort. As he struggled to pull it on, Lilly leaned and pushed it onto his foot.

"Thanks."

"You didn't answer my question."

"I don't know what time." He searched for the right words, a way to offer help without sounding like he was giving orders. "Stay here. I don't know what's going on with you or what you're running from, but you don't need to keep that little girl in a hotel."

"I can't just barge into your home."

"You're not barging. I have plenty of room and I've offered."

"I don't know."

"No strings, Lil," he promised, the same promise he'd made years ago. And she knew he had kept that one.

She glanced toward the kitchen where Shelby was still eating. The little girl lifted the glass of chocolate milk Kathy had given her and took a drink, leaving behind a milk moustache that she wiped away with her sleeve.

"She's a cutie, Lil, and she obviously needs stability."

Lilly nodded. "Yes, she needs that more than anything."

"So stay."

She looked down and then she nodded. "I'll stay." She turned toward him. "On one condition."

"What is it?"

"You can't keep trying to drag me into your life. I don't have time for games and you know how I feel."

"Yes, I know." He tried to smile. "You still have the same rule: no cowboys."

It had only taken him one proposal to understand how badly he didn't want to be spurned. He had spent a lot of years reminding himself that he wouldn't let that happen again.

"No cowboys," she repeated, without looking at him.

"Exactly. And you have to realize that I'm here to build a good life for Shelby. I'm going to fix up my house, get a job, and take care of my niece."

"I see. So you're back for good?"

"For now that's my plan. Unless things change."

He stood up, and she looked away. He knew that she was hiding something from him. For now he'd let her keep her secrets, but he would also make sure she stayed safe.

"I have to go, but I want you to know that you can stay

as long as you like. And when you decide to talk, I'm here. Friends are a good thing to have, Lil."

"I know." She finally looked up. "And I will let you know if I need anything."

She walked him to the front door and as they stepped out onto the porch, Johnny pulled up in his truck. Ian raised his right hand and waved to his foreman.

"There's my truck."

"Will you be okay driving?"

"Sure I will." He paused on the top step. "Have a good day. If you need anything, ask Kathy."

The door shut behind him as he walked down the steps of the porch and crossed to the driveway where Johnny waited for him. The old foreman shook his head and grinned.

"You're going to end up in so much trouble bringing her here." Johnny handed Ian his keys as he gave that bit of advice.

"I've been in trouble before."

"You should tell her everything before this goes too far."

Ian opened the truck door and stepped up into the four-wheel drive. "Probably should, but I'm not going to. Not yet. She's already decided what and who I am. I'm not sure if I want to change that. It might be easier this way, if she doesn't know."

"You've never let her know who you are. From the day you stepped off that plane years ago you've been pretending to be something other than what you are."

The lecture ran its course and Ian ignored most of it. He'd heard it before, too many times. Even if he agreed with Johnny, he didn't know how to go back and undo the past.

"She'll figure it out soon enough. If she's around here for long, it's bound to come out." He slipped the key into the ignition. "She's a nurse and she wants a job at the hospital."

"I guess it'll come out then. Maybe you should go ahead and tell her the whole story."

"Maybe."

"Stubborn kid." Johnny waved good-bye and shut the truck door.

Yes, stubborn. Ian had always been that. At seventeen he'd wanted to have fun, to be like every other kid. He had wanted to squeeze the joy out of life. He couldn't have done that if everyone had known the truth. Even though the truth might have changed Lilly's opinion of him.

CHAPTER 3

Ian walked through the fluorescent-lit halls of the Pediatrics Department. The rooms were quiet, and for the most part, dark. A nurse or an aide would occasionally pass, smile a greeting and move on.

It had been a fairly quiet night, after a busy day. At least the last hour or so had been quiet. He didn't care for busy days in his job. Busy days meant a child hurt, or sick. When he could save the life of a child, that made his day better.

He walked behind the counter of the nurses' station and sat down. A nurse, busy with a report, smiled in his direction but continued working.

He stretched both arms in front of him, and leaned forward. If he kept the muscles loose, he almost felt like a normal person.

"So, how's the shoulder?"

Ian raised his head and glared at the man who had walked up behind him. Dr. Devon Jacks sat down. The nurse forgot her paperwork and stared. Ian didn't get it, but that was just the reaction women had to Jacks.

Had to be a woman thing, because Devon's blue eyes didn't do a thing for him.

"Shoulder's fine." Ian reached for a folder that he wanted to look over. "How's life on the second floor?"

"Not too bad." Jacks moved away from the desk. Before Ian could react, the other man had grabbed his shoulder. Pain shot down his arm, and Ian jerked away.

"I said it's fine."

"I know what you said. You're going to end up needing surgery."

"Spoken like a surgeon." He rubbed at the tender joint. "But I don't plan on letting that happen."

"Better take care of yourself, then."

Ian stood up. "Yeah, I will. And now I have to get home."

As he stood up, his pager vibrated against his hip. He looked down, and shook his head.

"It looks like I won't be getting home for awhile, and I bet you won't either. They're bringing in victims from an MVA."

Multiple Vehicle Accident on a night like this, when rain came down in sheets, and the roads were slick from the combination of water and the oil that seeped up from the pavement.

Ian listened as he was paged over the intercom. He grabbed his stethoscope off the desk of the nurses' station, and headed toward the elevator.

The next two hours went by in a rush of activity as two children were brought in from the accident. One was kept in pediatrics, the other flown to Tulsa via helicopter.

Ian brushed a hand through his hair as he walked toward the room where the mother waited for news of her children. She had been admitted with a concussion that needed to be monitored. The father had been drinking. He walked away with no injuries. He would spend a night in jail. Hopefully longer.

He didn't want to think about that dad, not right now while his adrenaline was still at a high level and his temper—well, he had it under control for the time being.

At the door of room 105 he stopped, said a prayer for wisdom, and then walked into the dimly lit cubicle. The

woman in the bed turned her head in his direction. She
didn't smile. She couldn't, not with her jaw swollen the way
it was. He would lay odds that the bruised, swollen jaw and
the black eye weren't from the car accident.

"Mrs. Carter, I'm Dr. Hunt. I treated your children this
evening."

She cried silent tears that raced down her cheeks. Ian
touched her hand, and wished that being a doctor meant he
could take away all of her pain, not just the physical.

"Mrs. Carter, your daughters are going to be fine. Jenny
is upstairs and you'll be able to see her tomorrow. And
Annie is on her way to Tulsa."

He explained the extent of the child's injuries, assured
the mother that both girls would recover, and then he
paused, knowing the family wouldn't recover if something
else didn't happen.

"Mrs. Carter, your family needs help."

She nodded, and more tears fell. Ian leaned toward her.
She met his gaze with one that asked—no, it begged—for
help. A drunk wasn't the only one that had to hit rock
bottom; sometimes an abused spouse had to hit it as well.

"I'm going to send people to talk to you."

She whispered a hoarse, "Thank you."

"You're welcome. And now you get some rest."

"Jenny."

"I'll sit with her for awhile. She won't be alone."

His assurance gave the woman some peace. She closed
her eyes and Ian waited a few more minutes, making sure
that her sleep was sound before he turned to leave.

An hour later, Ian walked out of the hospital into the
downpour that had caused too many accidents that night.
Finally he could go home.

Home. And Lilly was there. He should have known

better than to get involved, but when it came to Lilly, he couldn't help himself. He made a promise to himself. He would help her through whatever was going on in her life, but he wouldn't let his guard down.

If she wanted a friend, that's what she would get—and nothing more.

A noise invaded the faceless dream, and Lilly woke up with a start. She rolled over on her back, waiting, listening. Had the noise been a part of her dream, or something innocent? Maybe beetles hitting the screen of the window? She didn't move; she couldn't. Fear held her as she played a game of what if.

It might be Carl down there now, trying to find Shelby. What if he had tracked them to Oklahoma? What if he took her niece away?

The clock on the dresser changed to 2:07 a.m. Lilly rolled out of the bed and reached for her robe. She slipped it on, pulled the blanket up around Shelby and tiptoed to the door. Before walking out of the room she grabbed a vase, the only thing that looked like a decent weapon.

At the bottom of the stairs she paused. Moonlight filtered in through the curtains and a shaft of pale light sliced through the living room. Nothing seemed out of place, but the hairs on her neck stood up in reaction to fear.

To her right something moved, and a shadow leapt across the opposite wall. Her heart thudded painfully in her chest before leaping into her throat to constrict her breathing. She lifted the vase, ready to do bodily harm.

"Are you going to hit me with that?"

The scream that rose up couldn't get past the lump of fear in her throat. So much for calm and courageous. She lowered the vase and leaned against the wall. Her legs shook and her heart raced. Taking calming breaths, she stared into the dark, looking for the owner of the voice.

She might still hit him with the vase.

"Where are you?" she whispered.

"Sitting here, in the alcove under the stairs." He sounded exhausted, and she took pity on him.

She moved away from the support of the wall and saw him sitting on a deacon's bench under the stairs. His mouth formed a tight smile and he winced. She sat down next to him and when she did, he reached for her hand.

His fingers, strong, warm, and slightly calloused from farm work, wrapped around hers. Lilly closed her eyes, and blocked a protest that rose to her lips. A quiet calm invaded her spirit as she sat there with him, knowing that she was safe. She couldn't protest or pull away, not yet.

"You're getting home late." She let go of his hand and moved hers back to the safety of her robe pocket. The other hand still held the vase.

"That happens sometimes." He closed his eyes and leaned back against the wall. "You aren't still planning to hit me with that, are you?"

"I might."

"Who are you so afraid of?" Concern edged his tone, and she knew that the look on his face would match.

Her resolve to remain independent and to keep him out of her life melted just a little. Having him care for her had always felt good. Once upon a time, Ian had made her feel special and protected.

"So, who are you afraid of?" he asked again.

"Other than you?" *The chaos you blend with stability in some haphazard way that I can't handle?* "Don't worry, I'm fine and I can take care of myself."

"Same old Lilly . . . same old mantra."

"Let it go, Ian." She stood up and put the vase on a nearby table. "Let me fix you something to eat."

She walked away and the groan behind her told her that he'd stood up. Pretending indifference to his pain wasn't easy. Knowing he followed, she walked to the kitchen. Flipping on the under-the-counter lights she moved to the refrigerator. When she turned, Ian sat at the island. He leaned on the granite top, resting heavily on one arm.

Lilly opened a cabinet and pulled out a glass. She filled it with water from the refrigerator and carried it to him. As she set it down, he looked up and smiled. The weariness around his eyes tugged at a part of her that she wanted to deny. Before she could stop herself she reached out and brushed at the stray hair that hung down across his forehead.

"Take something for the pain and I'll get your dinner. I saw a foil-covered plate in the fridge; Kathy probably left it for you."

"She usually does." He reached into his left pocket and pulled out a small bottle.

He struggled with the lid, fumbling with the child safety cap. She took it from him and twisted it off. When he held out his hand, she shook a pill into his palm.

"Thank you." He popped the white pill into his mouth and chased it down with water.

"Did you have someone check that arm tonight?" she asked as she took the foil off the plate and slid it into the microwave.

"No, I didn't have time. Don't worry, it's happened before. In a week it'll be as good as new."

"One of these days it won't be."

"Probably."

The microwave dinged and she took the plate out. "Pork chops and mashed potatoes. Kathy is a great cook." She put the plate down on the island top. "I remember when she used to invite me in to eat with them. Those are the memories of my childhood that I treasure."

He had picked up the fork and stabbed at the meat. He wouldn't ask for help. Silly male pride.

Lilly slid the plate out from in front of him and cut the meat.

"How did you do your job tonight?" She finished cutting the meat and slid the plate back in front of him.

"I was fine most of the night, as long as I kept moving and didn't let it get stiff. It didn't really start to tighten up until the drive home."

"You didn't use the sling?"

"No."

"You need a keeper." Scolding made her feel better. "I guess that must be Kathy and Johnny's job. It certainly isn't mine."

"They've been good to me."

She stopped talking as he ate. When he finished she took the plate, rinsed it and put it into the dishwasher. After wiping down the counters, she turned and found that the medication seemed to be working already. He leaned forward in his seat, nodded and then opened his eyes. A grimace followed the action.

"You should go to bed. Can you make it?" Lilly touched his shoulder.

Ian opened his eyes and nodded. "Yeah, I can make it." He leaned forward again.

Lilly touched his shoulder and he hunched forward a little more, an invitation she couldn't ignore. She moved behind him and rubbed her palm across his back.

"Relax." She leaned and whispered the word in his ear. He mumbled something unintelligible.

Lilly moved her hands to his shoulders and massaged. She could feel the muscles relaxing and she kneaded gently, moving away from the spot that caused him to flinch each time she touched it.

"You're good at this." His head rolled forward. She caressed the back of his neck, running her fingers across the tanned flesh, and then she returned to his shoulders, massaging the knotted muscles.

"That should help. Go to bed. You'll regret it if you sleep there much longer."

She leaned, tempted by the back of his neck. One kiss wouldn't hurt. It wouldn't be their first. As if he sensed her dilemma, he turned, his whiskered jaw rubbing the back of her hand. The touch brought her back to reality and she pulled away.

"Thank you, Lilly."

"Good night, Ian."

"Lilly."

"Be quiet, Ian." She touched his shoulder and then stepped away from him in an attempt to make a clean break. "You've always been a big baby when it comes to pain."

"I'm not a big baby. I'm injured."

"Yes, and as a nurse, I'm telling you that you need a doctor."

He rubbed at his face and shook his head. "I'm tired, Lilly. I can't have this conversation with you tonight."

"We don't need a conversation. I'm just giving you my opinion." She walked away and left him sitting there. He called her name again, but this time she ignored him.

As Lilly walked up the stairs to her room, she called herself every kind of fool. But she reminded herself of one important fact. As dangerous as Ian might be to her convictions, she knew that Oklahoma was the best place for her niece.

Daylight streamed through the open curtains and a shaft of sunlight hit Lilly full in the face. She closed her eyes against the glare and tried to convince herself it wasn't really morning.

Maybe if she went back to sleep she would wake up in Kansas City, in her own apartment, and all of this would just be a dream. Ian would be nothing but a forgotten summer years ago. Carl would be in jail. She would be back in her world, with her schedule, three on and three off, once a week out with the girls from her Bible study, and Sundays in her church. Each day falling into place, in the pattern of existence she had set for herself.

"Make her trot again, Johnny."

That happy squeal shook Lilly from her false belief that her life had turned into a dream—a bad dream—that she could wake up from. She jumped out of bed and ran to the window. Peeking out, she saw her niece on the back of a gray pony. The animal started to trot, and the child on his back bounced precariously, while laughing loudly.

She closed the curtains and hurried to the closet for something to wear before running down the stairs. On her way to the back door she almost bumped into Kathy. The older woman smiled.

"Isn't that just the picture of a happy child?" Kathy nodded toward Johnny and Shelby. They had a clear view of the pair through the French doors in the dining area.

"No, it isn't. It looks dangerous." It looked like a trip to the ER with a broken arm. And it brought back memories of her father putting Missy on a half-wild colt and telling her to hold on. Lilly moved toward the door but a hand on her wrist stopped her progress. She turned toward Kathy.

"Don't ruin this for her, Lilly. Don't take away her happiness, or punish her because of what you went through."

Lilly took a deep breath and exhaled as she worked to deal with the pain that statement inflicted. Those words coming from anyone else would have made her mad. From Kathy they made sense.

It didn't undo the stab of something resembling jealousy that Lilly felt. How hard had she tried to bring that smile back to her niece's face? It had taken her forever. And with one ride on a pony, Johnny and Ian had her giggling like the happy child Lilly wanted her to become.

She couldn't be jealous of that. And she wasn't. Confusion assaulted her and she shook it off. First and foremost was Shelby's happiness, and her safety.

"I'm trying to let go, Kathy. I just . . ."

"Remember too much." Kathy patted her arm. "Let her ride the pony. Let Johnny and Ian have fun spoiling her."

"Are the two of you talking about me?"

Ian walked into the room from the direction of the utility room. For a moment Lilly forgot everything else, including her conversation with Kathy. The focus of her attention was Ian, his casual swagger in faded jeans, and that half-grin of his. With his hair still wet from the shower he looked too good, too tempting.

Lilly looked down, concentrating on the wood floor beneath her feet. A wish that it would open up and swallow her didn't come true.

"We would never talk about you," Kathy scolded. "Now let me get back to cleaning my kitchen. I don't know what you're going to do today, but Johnny and I are going to see Jamie and the baby after church. Tommy is still out on the truck and she's lonely."

Ian laughed. "Anything to see that grandbaby."

Jamie had a baby. Lilly felt left out. One of her dearest friends had gotten married and had a child. And Lilly hadn't known about those two all-important events. Not that it was Jamie's fault. The choice to leave and to not look back had been Lilly's.

"You'll have to get over there soon, Lilly. Jamie'll be looking forward to seeing you." Kathy's voice brought Lilly back to the present. She looked up with a start and smiled at the older woman.

"I'll get over there soon." Lilly's attention returned to the scene outside the window, where Shelby now stood on the ground, hugging the neck of the pony.

Ian touched her arm, and she pulled away. "It's a pony, Lilly. Don't let it upset you."

"She's all I . . ." Lilly cut off, shaking her head because she knew he wouldn't understand. "I'm her guardian, Ian. I want to keep her safe."

"I apologize." He finished buttoning his shirt and took a step toward the back door. "I'll have Johnny put the pony up. Would you like to go to church with me?"

"Not today."

"I understand. Maybe we can have lunch when I get back."

She nodded and looked up into hazel eyes that looked beyond the excuses she gave. He had questions. She could see it in that look. She had questions of her own, for him, and for this life that didn't seem to fit the rebellious boy she had known.

Ian handed her the sling he carried. "Do you mind?"

Of course not, she was a nurse. Nurses could remain detached when they needed to. She could pull on cool reserve like a cloak and pretend he was any other patient.

She took it from him and slipped it under his arm, and then pulled the straps up to his neck. As she adjusted it around his neck he turned to look at her, sending a wave of clean, masculine scents her way. The herbal smell of his shampoo blended with soap and after-shave. Lilly hurried to finish so that she could break the contact with him and remember that she was mad.

For the life of her, she couldn't remember why.

"I'm going to bring Shelby in for breakfast." She sputtered the excuse for her speedy getaway.

"She had breakfast an hour ago." Kathy moved through the room carrying a broom. "And you need to eat something before you get blown away by a good Oklahoma wind."

Lilly ignored the wink that Ian shot her way.

"I'll pick you up after church and we'll have a picnic at the lake," Ian offered.

Lilly nodded before she really considered what she had just agreed to. She started to recant but realized how silly that would be. Lunch at the lake; no big deal.

"Lilly, tell me what's going on. Where's Missy?"

Lilly walked into the kitchen and pulled milk out of the fridge. Ian stood a few feet away. She ignored his presence as she poured cereal into a bowl.

"I don't want to talk about it. Not yet. I came here to give Shelby a chance, and I don't want to make Missy's mistakes common knowledge."

"I understand, but it doesn't hurt to have friends."

"Friends tell each other everything. Is that what you're saying? Then why don't you tell me about what you do at the hospital and about this place."

Ian's smile dissolved. "We'll talk about it later. It's a long story."

"I like long stories." She moved past him to the island and pulled out a stool.

"I'm sorry." And he looked it. "It'll have to wait."

"Fine." She took a bite of Cheerios, and hoped he realized that the conversation was over.

He must have, because he shook his head, and then he walked away. Good. She wanted to be left alone.

CHAPTER 4

Lilly waited until Ian left, and then she loaded Shelby into the van and drove down the gravel road to her childhood home. She had avoided going down to look at it. For some reason facing that house meant facing the past, and her memories of her childhood. She had needed a few days to adjust to the idea.

Avoidance was over. As her car came to a stop in front of the square white house with its sagging front porch, she cringed at the task before her. She also questioned how she had ever considered this a good idea.

Shingles were missing from the roof. Vines crawled up the walls and covered the windows. Weeds had overtaken what used to be a fenced-in yard, but the fence had fallen and the lawn and fields had become one and the same.

A dozer might be more suited for the job than the broom, bottle of pine cleaner, and roll of paper towels that she had in the back of the van. Industrial strength or not, the cleaner wasn't going to cut the filth that she found when she walked through the front door of the house.

Shelby stood on the front porch peering inside, her thumb in her mouth, and her blue eyes wide with wonder. And possibly some fear. Spider webs hung like lace veils, and something brown scurried past her to hide in a hole in the corner of the living room. Lilly choked on a shriek that tried to escape. No need to let Shelby know that even she would consider sucking her thumb at that moment.

"Okay, this is good. Nothing a little cleaning won't help." Or a match.

"I want to go to Ian's house and ride the pony." Shelby ducked her head, and big tears dripped down her cheeks.

"I know, Shelby. I don't blame you for wanting to go back. But this is going to be our home. We can fix it up. You'll see."

Shelby looked up, obviously not convinced.

"I don't like spiders."

"Neither do I. But we'll get rid of the spiders."

And the mice. Probably a few snakes. A chill raced up her spine, raising the hairs on her arms as it ran its course. She'd almost prefer to be riding that pony herself.

But it could have been worse, the optimist hiding inside her, afraid of the mice but still hopeful, tried to counter. Ian had watched over the place, keeping it from falling into the ground. The posts supporting the front porch had been replaced. The windows were still intact. That left her with major cleaning and only minor repairs to take care of before she could move back in.

She could do it. A few nails, a hammer, some shingles, and it would be done. Flowers would be a nice touch, too. If she closed her eyes she could almost picture it, a fresh coat of paint and a trellis of climbing roses up the side of the porch.

As easily as she could picture the changes, she could also picture Ian there, helping. He would want to be involved. And she would have to set the boundaries to keep him from taking over.

She had Shelby to think of, and their new life to plan.

But of course, thirteen years ago she'd had Missy.

Once again she was starting over. But this time she was starting over in the house she had left behind.

"Come on, Shelby, let's see if there is still a garden spot. I used to grow watermelons when I was your age." She took the little girl by the hand and led her down the steps to the overgrown yard.

"I like strawberries," Shelby whispered as they tramped through grass that tangled around their ankles.

A sob tried to escape, but Lilly choked it back. A few tears slid down her cheeks, not mindful of how hard she tried to hold it together for her niece. But how could she hold it together when she felt like such a failure? Her four-year-old niece liked strawberries. Lilly should have known that simple fact.

What else did her niece like, or need, that Lilly didn't know? She had failed with Missy, now she seemed to be failing with Shelby.

"Aunt Lilly, why are you crying?" The sweet little voice cleared Lilly's thoughts and jerked her from doubts. She could do this. She was older now, wiser. And Shelby needed her.

"I don't know, honey. I guess just thinking about how much I love you. Remind me, and I'll get you some strawberries."

"Someday I want a pony." Shelby's voice had taken on a wistful tone. "And someday my mommy can come and ride my pony with me."

"She would like that." Lilly looked up, at the clear blue sky, and prayed. She wanted her sister back in their lives. But she wanted Missy whole, and happy.

Missy had cried the day they left this place, and for weeks following. Lilly hadn't understood that. She had been relieved to leave this behind. For her, leaving here had meant leaving behind a low-paying job at a truck stop, and the well-meaning sympathetic looks of the people in town.

In retrospect, maybe she should have listened to her sister. Maybe she shouldn't have been in such a hurry to get away.

Maybe Missy would have been okay, and Shelby would still have a mom if Lilly hadn't insisted on a fresh start. Maybe they could have made it work here. Or maybe not.

They were walking around the back of the old garage when she noticed tire tracks in the grass. Someone had been there recently.

Carl? Lilly didn't want to believe that it could have been him. Carl was on the run from the police. And he didn't know how to find this place. It could have been anyone. More than likely it had been teenagers looking for a place to party. Somehow she couldn't convince herself of that.

Instead she glanced around, hoping she wouldn't see Shelby's father watching them from behind a tree, or from a distant hill.

"Shelby, let's go inside. You can play your ABC game while I get started cleaning." Lilly led her niece into the house. She swept a corner clean, and spread a blanket on the floor. "Sit here, honey. I'll make a quick look through the house to see what we need to fix first."

Shelby sat down on the blanket and pulled the battery-operated game onto her lap. Her attention was immediately drawn into the music and beeping sounds of the toy, and everything else was forgotten. Oh, to be a four-year-old. Lilly wished she could put her troubles as easily from her mind.

Something didn't feel right, but nothing seemed out of place. She stepped outside and walked around the house, searching for something, but she didn't know what. Her heart beat with heavy thuds against her chest, and the stirring of leaves in the trees made her jump. She glanced around, looking, making sure that no one was around.

"Aunt Lilly." Shelby's screams sent a flash of hot fear coursing through her body. Lilly ran back to the house, her legs moving like lead weights had been attached to her ankles. She jerked the door open, glancing inside for any sign of danger. Her niece's tear-stained cheeks and red-rimmed eyes were the only evidence that something was wrong.

"Shelby, what's wrong?"

"I saw, I saw . . ." She hiccuped and cried harder.

"What did you see?"

"I saw a, a spider outside and it looked mean."

Lilly sank onto the blanket next to the little girl. She buried her face in her hands and tried not to cry, or laugh, or give way to the array of emotions that had plunged her nearly into hysteria.

The fact that Lilly's van was no longer in front of his house didn't surprise Ian. She had run, just as he had expected her to do. He knew that he had to take part of the blame. He had pushed. He hadn't meant to, but his natural instinct to take care of problems had pushed aside his good intentions to remain detached.

He sat in his truck, trying to think of where she might have gone. It hurt to think she might have left the area. Another thought, this one making more sense. She probably went down to work on the farm.

He shifted into reverse and backed out of his drive. In his rearview mirror he saw another car, just down the road and parked on the grass shoulder. As he backed out, the other car took off. Ian accelerated and zoomed down the gravel road in the direction of Lilly's farm.

The red van was parked out front. He breathed a sigh of relief when he saw Shelby in the yard under the shade of an oak tree. The little girl looked up, a small smile playing on the corner of her lips before her head ducked and she looked away. She had opened up since their arrival, but shadows of fear still lurked in her blue eyes. At times she seemed to want his attention, and other times, like now, she seemed to pull inside a shell.

Lilly walked through the front door and on to the porch carrying a broom. Her thick dark hair was pulled back in a ponytail, and dirt smudged her cheek.

Ian jumped down from the truck and walked up the path to the house. His mind took him back to his seventeenth summer and a girl in jeans and a T-shirt, thin and gangly but with a smile that lit up his world.

The first time he saw her she had been dressed a lot like she was at that moment, in jean shorts and a T-shirt. She had been crying that day, and her eyes had been rimmed with red. Even then he had felt a strong urge to keep her safe, and to make her feel cherished.

When it had become obvious that she didn't want to be protected, he had instead turned to finding ways to make her laugh and smile.

He seriously wanted to see that smile again, not these restrained versions that she was showing him. To see that smile, he would have to find out what had happened to bring these shadows to her eyes.

"I found you," he said as he climbed the steps.

"I wasn't hiding." She leaned the broom she carried against the porch rail. "Did you bring lunch?"

"I did. I stopped by KFC." He leaned against the post. "We were going to the lake. Remember?"

"Yes, I remember." She looked out at the fields. A light breeze swept through, picking up tendrils of her hair that had come loose and blowing them around her face.

"How does the old place look?" Ian edged back to sit on the rail.

"Dirty, very dirty. And inhabited by four-legged creatures

with beady eyes. I can get it clean, and we'll make it here until I can do something else. Thank you for looking after it."

"You're welcome, and I didn't mind." He glanced at Shelby, who was still playing under the tree. She was out of earshot, so now would be the best time. Now was the time for him to ask questions, and get answers.

"Lilly, there was a man sitting in a car up by my house."

The color washed from her face and she looked away, her gaze focusing on Shelby. Her hands trembled as she clasped them together in front of her.

"Who is he?"

She closed her eyes for a moment. When she opened them he could see that she had composed herself. She was in control, the way Lilly always was. She had a way of taking everything in stride. She faced the obstacle, made plans for how to deal with it, and continued to move forward.

"I can't help you if I don't know who he is and what's going on."

"How should I know? I didn't see him."

"No, but it's obvious you're running from something. You didn't come back without good cause. And you aren't this edgy for no reason. I want to help."

She looked up, brown eyes softening as a smile slid across her face. "I know, and I appreciate that. But I have to do this. I have to take care of Shelby."

"Fine, but if you need anything, I'm here."

She looked away, her gaze lingering on the blond-haired child in the yard. Her look changed, softening and yet becoming more determined.

"Thank you, Ian. I promise you this—if I need help, you'll be the first to know." She brushed her hands off on her jeans. "I'm going to call Shelby to wash her hands. We can sit here on the porch and eat. This is probably the cleanest place on the farm."

She wouldn't give him more than that, but he was okay with what she had given. It was a start. Not much of one, but it was something.

Lilly walked to the open front window and peeked out. Ian sat on the steps with Shelby. The two of them were sitting with their heads bent together whispering. It tugged at Lilly's heart. She had never seen Ian interact with a child. He had a gift. And Shelby needed a man in her life who would show her that some men were kind and decent.

Their conversation made her stop and listen, even though she hadn't planned to eavesdrop.

"Do you like it here, Shelby?"

The child nodded, dragging her finger through the layer of dust on the porch to make a circle. She looked up, blue eyes searching his face. Lilly leaned back, out of sight. She didn't want to see the pain in those blue eyes.

"I'm not scared."

Lilly swallowed, and brushed away the tears that welled up and dripped down her cheeks. If she had doubted the rightness of her choice to come here, she did no longer.

"But Aunt Lilly is sad, and I don't want her to be sad. I don't mind going home if she wants to go."

"She wants you to be happy, and safe, Shelby."

"I miss my mommy."

Lilly knew how that felt. Her own mother had been gone for nearly thirteen years, and she still missed her. At times she still wanted to feel those comforting arms, and to hear the words that it would all work out.

Her mother had always told her to stop worrying, and just trust the Lord to take care of it. "Don't do no good trying to solve life's problems on your own, girl. Not when God has a better plan than you can even imagine. Oh, Lilly, sometimes I worry that you'll miss His plan, out trying to create your own."

Lilly's mother had always managed to find faith, even when things were at their roughest. Only after Lilly's dad died did she seem to give up.

"Oh, Momma, I wish you were here." She whispered the words into the living room, empty of furniture and of possessions, but reminding her of that past life she had lived here.

"It will all work out." Ian's voice, and not her mother's. She peeked out the window and saw that his words were for Shelby, and his arm was around the child's shoulders, holding her close. And Shelby had allowed his touch. Shelby trusted him.

That made it all worthwhile. Whatever it cost Lilly, it was worth it if Shelby learned to trust, and to laugh. She left her place by the window and walked out the front door.

"What are you two up to?"

"Ian's telling me he'll let me have a p—"

"Purple ball," Ian finished. The two of them wore matching looks of guilt.

"Purple ball, my foot." Lilly sat down next to Shelby and took a bite of the mashed potatoes on her plate. "Finish your lunch."

Ian laughed, but he didn't fill her in on their conversation. Lilly didn't need to be told. She knew that pony started with P. And Ian planned on taking over.

P is also for protector. He had always had a Lancelot complex, charging to the rescue of all the fair damsels. Of course he only wanted to charge to the rescue if it meant sitting on the back of a horse.

Lilly started to get up, but stopped when a low rumbling noise reached her. She listened, hoping it was her imagination.

"What is it?" Ian stood up, and set his plate down on the porch rail.

"Nothing, I thought I heard a car." Cars didn't come this far back off the main road. On Jackson Creek Road there were only two places—Ian's and hers.

"I hear it too."

"It's probably on the highway." Lilly moved, but Shelby's head flopped. The child had fallen asleep against her.

"Lilly, tell me what's going on." Ian sat down, his tone lowering when he noticed the sleeping child.

"Not right now. I need to put her down. I have a blanket in the living room for her to sleep on."

She tried to move, to find a way to pick up her niece without waking her. Ian took matters into his own hands. He stooped in front of them and scooped Shelby up.

"I could get her," Lilly protested.

"And I've already got her."

She followed him into the living room and watched as he put Shelby down. Lilly picked up a blanket that she had draped over a folding chair. She spread it over her niece and then she stepped back outside.

Ian followed.

"So, who is it?" he asked.

Lilly sat down in the spot she had abandoned. Ian walked down the steps to the yard and then turned to watch her.

"I'm going after the man in that car."

"No!"

"Why not?" He had his keys out of his pocket.

"Because I don't know what he would do to you. I just

wanted to come somewhere safe. I wanted to give Shelby a chance to grow up in a normal environment, in a place where kids won't know that her mother is in prison. I wanted a place where she could eat chicken on Sunday, and be surrounded by people who care."

"Missy's in prison?" Ian took off his hat and wiped at the perspiration that beaded across his forehead. "I'm so sorry."

"It's my fault, so you don't have to be sorry."

He shook his head, obviously not getting it. "Your fault? How do you get that?"

"I took her away from here. I took her to the city, to a world she didn't understand. A world with too much temptation."

Ian sighed, and his look changed to one of sympathy. She didn't want sympathy, not when she felt this close to tears.

Closing her eyes, she waited until calm returned.

"She got involved with Carl, and Carl was a drug dealer. He had her out buying cold medicines from pharmacies, and helping him to deliver to his buddies. She was strung out, weighed almost nothing, and she was neglecting her daughter. She got caught and when she did, I convinced her to turn Carl in."

"Which is why he's after you." He sat down next to her, and reached for her hand. His fingers wrapped around hers and she didn't protest, not this time.

"Yes. He managed to escape from custody. And he's threatened to take Shelby from me. He doesn't want her. He just wants to punish us."

"We won't let him get her, or hurt you."

"There is no 'we' in this equation, except for Shelby and me. I'm not here for your protection, Ian. I'm here because as much as I don't want to be on this farm, I do want

65

Shelby to have a life that doesn't include gangs and drugs."

"You can't run from drugs." His softly spoken comment needled into her heart.

"I know that. I know that drugs are everywhere, but this place . . . as much as I wanted to fight it, this is home."

"And you have friends here."

"I have friends in Kansas City, too. I've done well for myself. I had a good job, and a nice apartment. Now I have a fast-dwindling savings account, an old farm, and the constant fear that Carl is out there somewhere. I'm so afraid he'll take Shelby from me and that I won't be able to find her."

"And you have friends who care. Before you get mad, just hear me out. Friendship isn't a threatening thing, Lilly."

"It is when I feel like you're trying to take over and be in control. I have to be in control, Ian. That's how I've survived all of these years. If I give up, if I rely on you or anyone else . . ."

"Somebody might let you down. It isn't about control, Lilly. You're afraid we'll let you down."

The old adage that the truth hurt had never been quite so clear to her. Lilly jerked her hand free from his and stood up. She walked away from the house and Ian followed.

"Don't try pop psychology on me. Go home, Ian."

"We won't let you down, Lilly. You should know that by now."

"I do know, but I have to build a life for Shelby. A home that is safe."

"I know."

She hugged herself, wishing she didn't have to hurt him to keep herself safe. All of her self-preservation instincts kicked into high gear. Just looking at him, at the strength he possessed—physically and spiritually—made her want to walk into his arms.

He stayed in one place, as if he knew her thoughts and thought she might take that one step forward. She couldn't. She even shook her head to answer the nonverbal question in his eyes.

He would be there for her if she needed him. But for now she needed to stand on her own. She needed to keep her heart intact and keep her mind on Shelby and on building a strong home that didn't include turmoil.

Ian reached for her, but stopped just inches from touching her arm. His hand dropped to his side. Lilly chewed on her bottom lip as he walked away with just a faint smile to say good-bye.

"Ian, I'm sorry."

He raised his hand, but he didn't turn. She watched him walk away, get in his truck and drive off. Once again she was alone. And that was what she wanted.

It just didn't feel like it at the moment.

CHAPTER 5

Ian cranked up the stereo, and Tim McGraw's voice singing about white tank tops and barbecue stains reverberated inside the cab of the truck.

He didn't stop at his house. He wasn't in the mood to go inside and pretend he was in a good mood, and that all was well in his world. It couldn't be, not when he was mad, a little confused and a lot fed up with Lilly Tanner.

She was the most stubborn woman he'd ever known. From the day she walked away, he had regretted ever meeting her. Shoot, he'd been regretting her longer than that. From the first time he'd showed up at his grandfather's farm, he'd had regrets of some form or other.

He had cared about her from the beginning, and by the time he had turned twenty, and she was eighteen, he had loved her. And then her mother had died, and she had escaped the life she had always resented.

He had helped her go because he had realized he couldn't keep her, not when she was so determined to find her own way. Nobody understood that better than he did. His own need to find his own way had led him to his grandfather's ranch in Oklahoma—far from the perfectly polished world of his parents and their plans for his life.

He and Lilly were a lot alike in that way. They had both escaped lives that seemed to be cast for them. Hers had been a life of poverty and struggle, with parents who had left the responsibilities of holding the family together to their daughter. His life had been about goals, and parents who had wanted more for him than he had wanted for himself.

The parking lot of the local building supply store was nearly empty. They didn't do a lot of business on Sundays. Ian pulled into a parking space and killed the engine on his truck, and Tim McGraw's voiced faded mid-sentence, as he was singing something about the return of a girl from his past.

The police car that pulled up next to him took him by surprise. He grinned when his friend Dean Stephens shook his head and pointed a finger at him.

"What's up, Dean?" he asked when the passenger-side window of the patrol car came down.

"I could ask the same of you." Dean pointed to the digits on his radar. "I should have pulled you over."

"I take it I was speeding?" Ian climbed down from his truck. He leaned in the window of the patrol car, resting his arms on the door.

"A little. What's up?"

Ian shrugged. "I'm a little worried. Lilly Tanner's back."

Dean laughed. "I guess that explains a lot."

"I'm glad you can be amused."

"It isn't my heart that's going to get trampled."

"Not this time, buddy. My heart is safe. She's a friend, and nothing more. And there's something up with her."

That got Dean's attention. He'd been a cop before he ever became one—always interested in solving a mystery. He leaned over, closer to the window. "What's going on with her?"

"Something about her sister's ex-husband and drugs."

"I'll check into it for you, and if I hear anything I'll let you know."

"Thanks, Dean. And now I need to order some roofing supplies and a couple of windows."

Dean tipped his hat. "Later—that is, if she lets you survive when she finds out you're fixing her house. And use the cruise control."

Ian laughed as he walked away, and he realized that he could laugh. Lilly was back. They could be friends, and he didn't have to be in control. He would live his life. She could live hers. He could be her friend.

And he told himself that what he was about to do wouldn't make her madder than a mare when you took away her foal for weaning.

A strange sense of sadness filled Lilly as she walked around the overgrown yard of her childhood home. Not all of her memories of this place were bad. A few good things had happened here. Her mother had loved her here. Her father had done his best.

Nights of sitting on the front porch, listening as her dad played the guitar and her mother sang. Those were the good memories—and probably her reason for coming back. She wanted to have times like that with her niece.

Long nights waiting up for her dad to come home, wondering how drunk he would be, or how much money he had won—or lost—at the rodeo . . . those were the bad memories.

The worst night, the night he hadn't come home. The night the bull had won, and her father had lost his life.

She had used anger to fight her sadness. It hadn't been fair for him to do that to them. It hadn't been fair for her mother to slip away into depression after his death, forgetting that she had two daughters who needed her.

Hunger hadn't been fair. Electric bills unpaid hadn't been fair. The looks on the faces of the people in the church when she'd asked them for help, that hadn't been fair either. She hadn't needed pity. She had needed food for her little sister.

Anger, old, full of bitterness, and so familiar, came creeping back. Lilly picked up a rock, gripped it in her fist and hurled it across the lawn. Tears fell then, hot and angry, racing down her cheeks in an unrelenting storm. It was safe to cry when people couldn't see.

It wasn't fair. Life wasn't fair. It wasn't fair that Missy was in jail and her worthless ex-husband was on the loose, running from the law. It wasn't fair that Lilly always had to be the strong one.

She was so tired of being strong, but she had to be. It took strength to hold her family together, to make it through tough times. It would take strength to raise Shelby.

Lilly's mother hadn't been strong, and she hadn't been able to face life.

The anger washed out of Lilly in the salty tears that coursed down her cheeks, leaving her as deflated as a forgotten party balloon. She sat down on the front porch and buried her face in her hands.

Somehow she would get through. If God had brought her home, He must have a plan. She had to believe that, or she wouldn't be able to make it. She had to believe that God hadn't brought her here just to forget her.

She reminded herself that even when the Israelites wandered in the wilderness, God remembered them. Even then, He took care of their needs.

The sound of a truck coming down the road, the tires humming on the pavement, caught her attention. She glanced up, and recognized Ian's red Dodge. For a moment she felt a twinge of something, somewhere in the region of her heart. She fought it back with the leftover feelings of anger that were so much easier to deal with.

The truck pulled to a stop and she met him as he climbed down, landing with a soft thud on the overgrown lawn. He pushed back his hat and looked over the house, fallen-down barn and overgrown lawn. He shook his head and turned his attention back to her.

"Why are you back so soon?" she asked.

"I brought you some supplies, and there'll be some men over here tomorrow to start working."

How easy it was to find anger when it was needed. Lilly shoved her hands into her pockets and gave him the look that would let him know that he had overstepped the boundaries.

"Who said I needed your help?"

"Nobody, I just wanted to help."

"It's my house, and I'll do my own repairs. I don't have the extra money to hire people and I'm not going to let you do it for me."

"Why can't you let people into your life?"

"Because I can't . . ." She didn't have a better answer than that. At least she didn't have an answer she could explain to him. "I have to do this myself."

"Fine."

"Fine."

He started to walk back to his truck. Halfway there he stopped and turned. "Lilly, why not put the past behind us?"

"This isn't about the past. This is about now. You have to respect my boundaries."

"Which are?"

She bit down on her bottom lip as she met his clear hazel gaze. He started to smile, she could see his lips tilt, but the look dissolved before it could be completed. Smart man.

Her boundaries. She needed them, for Ian and for herself.

"Friendship is fine, Ian. But you can't take over my life.

You have to let me take care of myself and Shelby. I've been a big girl for a long time."

"You've been a big girl forever."

She looked away, unwilling to see the compassion reflected in his expression. Sometimes she felt like she had been an adult her entire life.

"I'll try to respect your boundaries," he promised. "If you'll try to let us into your life once in awhile. I'll respect your boundaries and I won't push, if you'll agree to stay at the ranch until you have this place ready to move into."

He held out his hand and she stared at it for a minute before realizing he meant for her to shake on it. Gathering her resolve to remain detached, she took his hand in hers and shook.

"Deal," he smiled with a wink to punctuate the gesture.

"Deal." She didn't feel like smiling.

"So, what do you plan to do around here?" Ian asked the question as if it didn't matter. He was trying to pretend he didn't care, and that he didn't want to charge in and take over.

She wanted to hug him for making that gesture.

"I don't really know. And I do know that the roof needs to be fixed. If you leave the roofing materials, I'll buy them from you and figure out what to do next."

"Okay, I can do that."

She glanced sideways, knowing that it cost him to say that, to agree to let her do this herself.

"So, can I have a look around?" He shoved his keys back into his pocket.

Lilly shrugged. "Sure, why not."

They walked to the back yard. Lilly surveyed the property with a critical eye, noticing more things that needed repairing. The chicken coop had a few boards that needed replacing, and the paint had faded, leaving gray, weathered boards. The garden plot hadn't seen a garden in years. Weeds, grass and flowers grew together in a jumbled mess.

"You might consider tearing that house down and re-building."

"Maybe." She walked over to the chicken coop and opened the door. Ian peeked over her shoulder. She was very aware of him leaning in behind her, even though he didn't touch her.

"You can raise chickens."

"I could. It might be nice to have fresh eggs."

Lilly turned away from the chicken coop. She shoved her hands into her back pockets and surveyed the work ahead of her. It would take time, but she could do it.

"I have to go to work for a few hours." He reached to pick a few late roses that had continued to grow in the jungle of a yard. Her mother's flower garden. Lilly felt a twinge in the region of her heart.

He handed her the flowers.

"Thank you." She lifted the red blooms to inhale the sweet fragrance. She remembered how the scent of the flowers used to drift into the house carried by soft summer breezes through the open windows. The cheap white cotton curtains would flutter, and the smell of pine cleaner would linger after her mother mopped.

"I need to go. Will you be okay?" Ian's hand was on her back as they navigated a rough patch of ground.

"Yes, I think so."

Ian walked her to the front porch. "Will you be at the ranch for supper? Kathy will be expecting you."

"I'll be there. I can't do much more around here, not without electricity."

"You have a cell phone if you need us."

"Yes, I do." She leaned and kissed his cheek. "You're a good friend."

"Yes, a good friend." He sighed, and she knew what he meant, that he wanted more. Friendship would have to be enough.

Ian stomped through the barn a few minutes after leaving Lilly. He picked up a discarded feed sack and tossed it into the trash barrel. When he turned, he realized he had company.

"What's got you all riled up?" Johnny leaned against a stall, a piece of straw sticking out of his mouth.

"Nothing. I just have a lot to get done around here and I wish I had more than a weekend to get it done."

"You know better than to lie." Johnny took a step away from the stall door he'd been leaning on. "Is she coming back up here? Or is she going to try and stay in that place?"

"That place isn't livable. She'll be back up here later. But she's determined to move in there."

Johnny rubbed his bushy gray eyebrows and shook his head. "Lilly, I-can't-stand-the-country, Tanner wants to live down at that old farm? I hope she thinks long and hard about that before she throws money into that place that she can't get back."

"It's her money and her farm."

"Is that what has you so riled? Son, you know you can't control her. She has to make her own decisions." Johnny followed him through the stable.

"I think I know that."

"She's a spunky thing, isn't she?"

"Yep." A buckskin head nudged Ian's arm when he stopped to pick up a piece of baling wire. He straightened back up and reached to pat the horse's neck.

"That horse needs to be ridden," Johnny informed him.

"He does, but it'll have to wait. I need to see if I can get that Caldwell boy down here a couple of times a week to exercise a few horses."

"He'd do it. He's horse crazy, and he needs something to keep him out of trouble. Boys are like that."

Ian knew all about boys in trouble. He'd been one, until he came to live with his grandfather for a summer. He had stayed for that summer, and sixteen more.

He had always hoped that Lilly would come back. Now he wondered why. His peaceful existence here had disappeared the day he saw her at the grocery store. It didn't look like it would be back any time soon.

CHAPTER 6

Two days later Lilly lugged her suitcases down the stairs of Ian's house and out to her van. Kathy stood in the doorway, hands on her hips and disapproval clearly imprinted in the lines of her face. Lilly ignored the look and tried to convince herself that she was doing the right thing.

The house had been cleaned out, and electricity turned on. She had no reason to remain in Ian's home. And with Ian at work, it seemed like the best time to leave.

Shelby sat on the front porch, looking not so positive about leaving. The child wore a look that matched Kathy's. That meant Lilly didn't have a single soul on her side. She looked up, wondering if even God was on her side, or if He was siding with Kathy as well.

"Come on, Shelby, time to go."

"I don't think we'll have chocolate chip pancakes." The little girl bit down on one corner of her lip and narrowed her eyes. The look, identical to the one Missy had used, made Lilly smile, and she didn't feel like smiling.

"We'll get the stuff for pancakes."

"Chocolate chip?" Shelby didn't look convinced.

"Yes. And chocolate milk, too."

Shelby stood up. "Can I still ride the pony? And even go to Sunday school with Kathy?"

"Yes, you can." Lilly walked up the sidewalk and took her niece by the hand. "We're not moving to Mars, Shel."

"I don't think I would like Mars." Shelby looked up, worry furrowing her brow as if she thought her aunt might really do something crazy like move them to outer space.

"We're not moving to Mars. We're just moving down the road."

Kathy took Shelby by the other hand and walked to the van with them. She remained silent, un-lecturing. She had been this same way all those years ago when Lilly had informed them of her need for a fresh start, somewhere far from the farm. Kathy had kept her opinions to herself, hadn't lectured or told her that her decision was the wrong one.

This time Lilly almost wished Kathy would say something, even if Lilly didn't agree. Part of her wanted to hear Kathy say that she shouldn't go.

And the stronger part of her knew that no matter what Kathy said, she would have to go. She couldn't stay with Ian, in his home, feeling as if he controlled her life and her future—and feeling like she wanted him in her future.

Ian had his farm, his horses and bull riding. And Lilly didn't want to be second to any of those things. She had grown up in a family where they all came second, with rodeos and bulls coming first. When she found a man to love, she wanted to be his priority, not just the woman he came home to after the rodeo ended.

Ian glanced at the clock on his dash and sighed. It was after midnight, and he felt every hour of the day knotted in the muscles of his back. He hit the button on the garage door opener, but something stopped him from pulling forward.

A flash of light. It could have been lightning in the distance. He might have considered that, but there wasn't a cloud in the sky. He waited, staring into the dark night. He saw it again, a flash of light down the road from his house.

He eased his truck back out of the drive and turned off the lights as he headed down the road in the direction of Lilly's place.

Lilly inched along the wall of the living room, her heart thudding in her chest, her hands clenched at her sides. She'd seen the flash of light; it had even flashed through her bedroom. It was that brief flash that had shaken her from a nightmare.

In her dream Missy had been crying for her, asking her for help. Lilly brushed away the tears that the memory of the dream evoked. She hadn't been able to help her sister.

"Lillian, open the door, sweetie, let me in."

Her body shook so hard she couldn't move. She couldn't unclench her fists. The nightmare had become reality, her worst fear. Even if she screamed, nobody would hear. The taunting voice called her name again, and then he laughed.

"You thought you could hide, but you can't. Remember this, Lilly: I could come in if I wanted. I could step right through this door."

The roar of an engine ended his taunting. Lilly sank to the floor, her back against the paneled wall. Headlights flashed across the room. Lilly allowed herself to breathe again. As her body trembled with the remains of the fear, she wrapped her arms around her middle and cried.

"Lilly, open the door." The doorknob rattled and the wooden door shook on its hinges. Lilly couldn't stand up, not yet. Her mind still heard Carl's sneering laughter and refused to believe that it was Ian.

"Lilly, it's me. Open the door."

She stood up, her legs trembling like reeds in the wind as she crossed the room. "I'm coming."

"Are you okay?"

"Oh, I'm wonderful." She twisted the dead bolt and the door unlocked.

As she swung the door open, Ian stood there in the opening, tall, strong and familiar. Her best intentions to be strong, to be independent, almost flew away. A big part of her wanted to fall into his arms for comfort. Somehow she held it together.

"Come inside, I don't know where he went."

"I saw him run off into the field. I wanted to check on you before I went after him."

"I'm fine. He's going to have to do more than that to get to me." She hoped her words were stronger than the trembling in her legs.

"I'm going to look for him." He stepped back out of the house. "Lock the door, and don't open it until I come back."

"Ian, don't."

"Lilly, I'm not allowed to tell you how to live. Don't tell me what to do. I'm going to find Carl. He's not going to do this to you."

"He's gone."

"He could still be out there."

He could, she realized. And he could come back while Ian was gone. A tremor raced through her at that thought. She reached for Ian, but let her hand stop short of actually detaining him.

"I'll be back." He leaned and kissed her cheek. "Lock the door."

She nodded and then he was gone. She shut the door behind him and locked the dead bolt. In the still night his truck engine roared to life. Lilly stepped to the window and watched as he drove off through the field, circling the house, and then expanding the search into a wider circle.

"Aunt Lilly, I'm scared."

Lilly spun around, her gaze landing on the child standing behind her. Shelby ran across the room and wrapped her arms around Lilly.

"There's nothing to be afraid of." Lilly didn't like the lie, but what could she tell the little girl? How could she tell a child that her own father was threatening her life?

"But I heard the noise outside my window," Shelby cried against Lilly's shoulder.

Lilly grabbed her niece up and ran to the bedroom. The window was open, and the screen was gone.

"Shh, Shelby, it's okay, there's nothing here."

"Aunt Lilly, I want to go home."

"I know, honey, but this is where we live now." Lilly held Shelby against her as she stepped cautiously toward the window and slammed it down. She twisted the lock, and then hurried out of the room.

Headlights flashed across the room again, and a car door slammed. Lilly tiptoed to the window, knowing it wasn't Ian. The engine had been too quiet for Ian's big diesel. Blue lights flashed across the lawn.

"Officer." She opened the door, and then as she recognized a familiar face she cried, "Oh! Dean."

"Lilly, Ian called. He's circling the property. He wanted me here with you."

"He's still here, Dean. He opened the window."

Dean flipped on a flashlight, his stern expression growing even more so. "Lock the door."

Lilly nodded as she closed the door, shutting out the night noises, and the sound of Ian's truck in the distance. So much for being strong and doing this on her own.

She whispered a quiet thank you to God for sending friends, and for keeping them safe.

81

Ian drove across the back of the field, out an open gate and down a dirt road that led to the highway. At least he knew how Carl had gotten in. There were still fresh tracks in the grass.

But no sign of Carl.

He turned left onto the road that would lead back to Jackson Creek Drive. In the distance he saw the flashing blue lights of Dean's patrol car, and he breathed a sigh of relief. Lilly wasn't alone.

When he pulled up in front of the house, he saw Dean walking around the yard with a flashlight. Ian climbed out of his truck and approached the other man.

"Anything?" he asked.

"Footprints. She's shaken up. He opened a window."

"Great." Ian exhaled, angry with himself for not doing more and with Lilly for being stubborn. "I'm going to drag her back to my house, if I have to take her kicking and screaming."

"That's abduction. It probably isn't safe, either. Have you ever grabbed hold of a half-wild barn cat?" Dean didn't laugh, but Ian heard the dry humor and he chuckled.

"Yeah, I suppose it is illegal and dangerous, but I can't have many nights like this."

"Does she know?"

Ian shook his head. Did she know about his job? No, and he wasn't looking forward to telling her.

"Not yet. I started to tell her, but she got mad about something else. And today I didn't get a chance."

"Sure."

"I get enough lectures from Kathy without getting them from you."

Dean flashed his light across the yard and it struck the

chicken coop. The door swung on its hinges.

"That wasn't open today," Ian whispered.

Dean nodded, pulled his gun from its holster and took a step forward. Ian followed a few steps behind. He hung back and Dean flashed a light into the doorway and kept his gun aimed inside the chicken coop. He backed out after a quick scan of the interior.

"Nothing here."

"He was there."

"Probably. But he's gone now." Dean flashed his light toward the house. "What do we do with her?'

"I already told you."

They walked back to the house, which lay in darkness. Lilly peeked out a window, her face pale in the moonlit night. Ian lifted his hand to wave.

"She's not going peacefully." Dean holstered his gun as they walked up the steps. "I'm not helping you."

"Didn't think you would. But I need to get some sleep and I won't sleep if she's here."

Lilly walked out the front door and met them on the steps. Ian joined her on the porch. Dean, the big chicken, remained in the yard, and Ian didn't blame him.

"He's gone, Lilly," Dean assured her. "But you shouldn't stay here."

"Don't take his side, Dean." Her arms were wrapped around her waist and she shivered.

"Lilly, you can't stay here." Ian kept his voice tempered, trying hard to sound like a friend and not the he-man she didn't want him to be.

"I can and I will stay here. This is my home. I want to raise my niece here. I can't let him run me off." She glanced in Dean's direction. "So I would recommend that you go find him, because I'm not leaving."

"Don't get mad at Dean, I'm the one who thinks you should leave." Ian brushed his hand down her arm. "Let's go inside and talk. It's getting cold out here."

"I'm not cold."

"If I said it's daylight, you'd argue about that."

She smiled and shrugged her shoulders as she stepped into the house ahead of him. "You're probably right."

Dean remained on the porch. Ian held the door open for him, but let it close with a soft thud when he realized Dean was talking into the microphone on his collar. With the teasing glint gone from his eyes, he joined them in the living room a moment later. "I have to go, I have another call holding. I'll keep an eye out for him."

"Thanks Dean." Ian extended a hand. "She'll be at my house tonight. At least until we can figure out how to keep her safe."

"This is my . . ."

Ian cut her off with a shake of his head. Suddenly exhausted, he didn't feel up to an argument with her. "Yes, it's your home. I think we know that. But your reason for coming back was for Shelby, not to prove to us all how strong and independent you are."

She blanched as if his words had dealt a physical blow. Ian couldn't take it back, not when her safety was at stake.

"Just come to the house for a night or two. You can get a security system out here, and then we'll all rest easier. But until then, you have to stay safe and keep Shelby safe."

Lilly looked out over the moonlit fields and nodded. "I guess you're right. I want Shelby to be safe."

Ian didn't feel as if he had won. He had got his way, and Lilly would be safe, but at what cost?

The bedroom at Ian's felt like a safe abode, and Lilly

didn't want it to feel that way. Or maybe she did. It soothed her with warm autumn colors, rich fabrics and soft rugs woven from alpaca wool. Funny, but it felt like coming home.

She shouldn't have been in such a hurry to leave. Now she could see that. But when she'd packed her bags and left, that had felt like the right thing to do. She'd come home to live in her old farm, not Ian's house.

She pulled the blanket over her niece and dropped a kiss on her forehead. The little girl didn't stir, but a small smile lifted one side of her rosebud mouth. Even Shelby felt more secure here. Lilly sighed at that thought.

On her way out of the room she squared her shoulders in determined resolve. She would stay until she felt it was safe to live at the farm. For now pride had to take the backseat. Ian needed to know how much she appreciated him.

She would . . . Her thoughts stopped rumbling through her mind when she entered the living room and found Ian sound asleep on the couch. He had kicked off his boots. One arm hung off the couch in a lifeless pose and a soft snore rumbled from his parted lips. He looked like a care-free kid. She knew better. During his waking hours, lines of concern furrowed his brow, and tenderness warmed his golden brown gaze.

Her heart clenched and tugged her forward. She tiptoed across the room and dropped to her knees next to the couch. He stirred, opened his eyes and smiled. If she could have moved, she wouldn't have, not at that moment when common sense fled, and her only thought was of Ian and all that he had done for her. He continued to be a friend, even when she didn't realize she needed his friendship.

His hand came up, caressing her cheek, and then tangling in the hair at the back of her neck. Her good sense seemed missing in action, and she had no desire to move away.

Ian sat up, his hands had moved to her shoulders and he pulled her close. As his mouth lowered to cover hers, Lilly shut her eyes and pushed thoughts of escaping far from her mind.

That first moment, when his lips touched hers, time stopped. Or maybe it took them back in time, to another moonlit night, and another kiss.

Lilly no longer wanted to run or escape. She wanted to be in Ian's arms, to be held close and to be protected. She reached up, touching his shoulders with tentative fingers, lingering for a moment in his arms before returning to the surface, back to reality.

She had left home thinking she would leave these feelings behind. And the feelings had been here waiting for her, knowing she would return.

"Lilly?" Ian's voice, his breath near her ear.

"We can't do this." Lilly sat back on her heels, breaking the physical connection between them, but still very aware of the other connection, the invisible bond that seemed infinitely attached.

"We're not doing anything." Ian moved, and took her hands in his. He lifted one, and then the other to his lips. "I have convictions too. I guess that isn't the most manly statement you could have heard from me. But this is as far as it goes."

It dawned on her then, what he had meant that first night by "I've never . . ." Her heart expanded with emotion that only moments before she had tried to squash.

"Ian, I . . ." She didn't know what to say, or how to say it.

"Don't, Lilly. I didn't tell you that to try to draw you

into my life. The decisions I've made are mine, between God and myself."

Hazel eyes locked with hers, asking for understanding and nothing more. Lilly nodded as she pushed herself to her feet. The distance between them brought clear thinking to the situation.

Lead us not into temptation. Either she thought it, or Ian whispered it. She didn't know which, but she knew that temptation could lead them both where they didn't need to go.

"Good night." But it wouldn't be a good night for either of them. It would be a night when she questioned her sanity, her reasons for returning to Oklahoma, and the feelings in her heart that couldn't be denied.

Lilly climbed the ladder with another load of shingles. The muscles in her back protested, but she ignored them. Rain had been predicted and she didn't want water pouring into the house, even if she wasn't staying there.

The fact that she was staying with Ian didn't sit well with her. She needed to start her new life here, and that meant moving into her own home. If she got the roof done, that would be a step in the right direction. If she could finish this one thing, maybe she would be able to convince herself that staying was a viable option.

The second step would be when the security people showed up in two days to install her new alarm system. She hadn't told Ian about the appointment. But she felt good about it. She needed to do this for herself, and Ian needed to see that she hadn't come home for his protection.

The familiar sound of Ian's diesel engine rumbled down the drive ahead of the appearance of the red truck. She glanced up the road and groaned. Sure enough, there it came. Kathy had ratted her out. Of course she had. Kathy was on Ian's side.

Lilly placed the shingles, grabbed roofing nails out of the pouch tied around her waist and started to pound. If Ian expected her to run to him or anyone else for help, he was wrong. She'd spent her childhood working on this farm. She knew how to patch a roof, fix a fence and repair plumbing.

Ian pulled his truck under the shade of the oak, next to her van. He stepped out, pulled his ball cap on, and headed toward the house. Lilly pretended she wasn't watching.

"You're the most stubborn female I've ever met."

"Let's play nice," she called down to him. "I don't have time to argue. I want to get this done before the rain sets in."

She looked up at the sky, hoping he would get the hint. He followed her glance, and had to notice the clouds gathering to the south.

Lilly went back to her work. The ladder shook and she knew that he was on his way up. She ignored his presence on her roof, even when he grabbed the extra hammer and held out his hand.

"Some nails, please." He waited, hand out. Lilly reached into the pouch and pulled out a handful. He took them from her, offering a smile and a wink.

"Don't you have a job?" She pounded a nail into the roof. "I don't want to get you fired."

"It's my short day. My partner . . ."

"Your what?" She sat back on her heels and waited for an explanation. One didn't seem to be forthcoming. Ian wasn't a stranger to roofing, and as she sat waiting, he moved on up the roof.

"Better hurry. It's going to rain," he called back, a few

nails stuck in the side of his mouth as he worked.

Lilly pulled a few more nails out of the pouch and went back to work, but her mind was now on the odd comments Ian made from time to time, and not on patching a leaking roof.

"I just felt a drop of rain." Ian pulled off his ball cap and looked up at the sky.

"I felt it too." She grabbed another stack of shingles and placed them on the next section of roof.

"Lilly, we can't stay up here in a storm. I need to run over to Jamie's. Do you want to go?"

She hammered one last nail, finishing the row she was working on. "Yes, I would like to go. But I need to check on Shelby."

"I already checked with Kathy. She's happy to watch her. Don't worry, she won't let anything happen. And Johnny is there to make sure of it."

"I know they'll watch her."

Lilly shoved the hammer into the pouch and scooted over to the ladder without looking back at Ian. She climbed down, and when she landed on the ground she grabbed the ladder and moved it away from the roof.

"Excuse me, I need that ladder." Ian sat on the edge of the roof, feet dangling over the side.

Lilly ignored him as she cleaned up the mess on the ground. She shoved old shingles that she'd torn off into a trash can, and then picked up some papers she had thrown on the ground.

"This could be funny if it wasn't about to storm."

She didn't look at Ian, but she looked up. Sure enough, rain was headed their way. The dark gray band was less than a quarter of a mile away. She could already smell the clean scent of rain. She held on to the ladder and turned to gaze at the man on her roof.

He looked sort of cute up there, ball cap pushed down on his head and a frown on his normally smiling face. And in a minute he would be soaked. She was pretty sure she didn't feel sorry for him.

"Lilly, come on."

"Okay, you get the ladder, but you have to hear me out."

"Like I have a choice." He smiled, so she wasn't too worried about him getting back at her.

"Stop treating me like I'm a child. I'm a grown woman and very capable of taking care of myself." She ignored a thread of guilt, or whatever it was. "Okay, fine, I am glad you showed up last night. But you have to remember that I can take care of myself."

He looked toward the south, and the rain. "Lilly, you're an adult and you can take care of yourself."

She pushed the ladder back to the house and he climbed down.

"And you're also a royal pain."

"I aim to please."

The rain hit, pouring down on them as they ran toward his truck. Ian beat her and was waiting in the cab when she reached the passenger side. She grabbed the door handle and yanked, breaking a fingernail in the process.

"Ian, unlock the door." She pounded on the window and he waved. The window came down an inch.

"How does it feel, Ms. Smarty Pants?"

"Like the shower I didn't want." She grabbed the door. After another yank she heard the lock click. She threw the door open and climbed inside.

"Thank you, Mr. Wonderful, I'm thoroughly amused."

"I just wanted you a little repentant."

She shook her head, and brushed away the trickle of rain

that dripped down her face. "I'm not repentant, just soaked."

She started to laugh as she brushed wet hair back from her face. Ian shot her a questioning look.

"So, now you think it's funny?"

"It was kind of fun, watching you up on that roof. I had forgotten that you're afraid of heights."

"Not afraid, just cautious."

"Scared to death. Admit it."

"Never, sweetheart, not in a million years would I give you that power over me."

Ian turned the truck around and headed up the hill. His smile disappeared and he glanced in her direction. "Lilly, I really don't know if it's a good idea for you to come down here alone."

"Ian, it also isn't a good idea for you to tell me what to do. I can't sit in the house every day, wondering where Carl is, and wishing I still had a life."

"Getting a little stir crazy, are we?"

She glared at him, "Yes, Ian, stir crazy. Can we forego lectures and advice for a few minutes?"

He didn't comment and Lilly assumed it was because the lectures were over. She breathed a sigh of relief that was short-lived.

"The police found a knife when they came over here this morning to look around." Ian's words fell into the silence of the truck. A song about a long black train played on the radio. She sometimes felt like she was on the train and heading in the wrong direction.

She looked out the window, ignoring his concerned glances. It took a few minutes to come to terms with one important fact: Ian wasn't the one stealing her independence. Carl was.

Until Carl was behind bars, neither she nor Shelby could be safe. As much as Lilly wanted to take care of herself, she wouldn't let her pride put Shelby in danger. If that meant staying with Ian for a few days, she would stay.

CHAPTER 7

The rain had stopped by the time they reached Jamie's house. Lilly looked up in wonder as the gray clouds parted and early evening sunshine broke through in shafts of golden light.

"Beautiful, isn't it?" Ian pulled the truck up the drive and parked in front of the brick ranch-style house.

"Yeah, it is. I've been in the city for so long, I guess I had forgotten how lovely it is out here."

"That happens." He stopped the truck and pulled the emergency brake. "Have I told you that I'm glad you're home?"

"I think you did." She reached for the door handle and pushed the door open. "There's Jamie."

The front door of the house flew open and Jamie, still as fresh-faced as she'd been in high school, came out the door. She still had brown curly hair like her mother's, and her father's big smile. Lilly climbed down from the truck and ran to greet her friend, accepting her welcoming hug and forgetting that it had been fourteen long years.

"Lilly, it's about time you got over here to see me."

Lilly didn't miss that Jamie's eyes glanced over her shoulder to Ian. She felt as if she was the center of some deep secret that everyone else shared.

"I'm just sorry that I haven't kept in touch."

"And you should be," Jamie scolded in her good-natured way, letting Lilly know that she held no hard feelings. "Come inside, have some iced tea and tell me everything."

"That sounds great."

Jamie looked past her again, and this time Lilly turned as well. Ian still stood behind them, his hat pushed back on his head, dark glasses covering his eyes.

"That rotten colt is in the corral, and I think you'll find that he's starting to act like he might be worth more than a plugged nickel," Jamie informed him.

"So you're telling me to go play with the horse and leave you two girls alone so that you can talk about me?" He laughed as he walked away. "I can't get a break around here."

"Lucky you didn't break that arm. Does that make you feel better?" Jamie called after him.

He laughed, but he didn't stop to return the friendly banter. Lilly watched him stroll off, the slow swagger of a cowboy learned to perfection over the years. He was even getting a little bow-legged from too much time in the saddle. On Ian it was sort of cute.

"Well, stop starin' if you don't want him to know you like him, and come in here and tell me why you thought it would be okay to leave us and not look back." Jamie took her by the arm and led her into the cool darkness of her home. "And be quiet, I just got my little darlin' to sleep. That takes a miracle most days."

They sat on the back deck of the house, under the shade of a big oak tree. Lilly sipped from tea that was too sweet, but very cold. Jamie drank water because caffeine kept the baby awake.

Lilly felt an emptiness grow like a deep ache inside her heart. Babies, husbands, houses on quiet lanes—everything she had thought she didn't need. And now thinking of those things, and seeing them up close, filled her with longing.

"Tell me where you've been and what you've been doing. Let me live a little through your eyes," Jamie pleaded, joy that belied the words sparkling in her gray eyes. She pushed a plate of cookies in Lilly's direction.

"I doubt very seriously if you would give this up for an apartment in Kansas City," Lilly scolded.

"On most days I wouldn't. Now there are mornings when the baby hasn't slept, and I haven't slept, and Tommy is gone, and on those days I'd like something different. Like maybe a new job for my husband."

"I don't blame you."

"But I don't want to talk about me. I want to talk about you," Jamie prodded.

"I went to college, got a job as a nurse, and now I have Shelby." Life in a condensed nutshell. It sounded so simple, when really it was anything but. She had gone from single, having a career, to suddenly being a single parent without a job.

"Where's Missy?"

Lilly knew she didn't mean to pry. The innocent question was probably one that everyone wanted to ask. It also made it obvious that Ian had kept her secret.

"She's in prison."

Jamie's hand reached to cover hers. "I'm so sorry, Lil. I guess I knew it would take something big to bring you back. I didn't dream it was something like that."

"You had no way of knowing, Jamie. And I really don't want it to be common knowledge. I don't even know why I came back here."

To that Jamie smiled and patted her hand. "You might fool some people with that, Lilly. You might even fool yourself. But you and I both know why you came back." She nodded toward the barn. "That guy out there with his cute little knees peeking through the rips in his jeans, that's why you're here. Even when we were sixteen you were in love with his knees."

95

"I'm not sixteen anymore. I know that it takes more than cute knees, more than a smile that makes your heart flutter. Not that those things aren't great, but it takes more."

"Yeah, too true. He's one of the sweetest guys I know. Not as sweet as Tommy, of course, but he is a pretty decent catch."

"I'm not looking for fish."

"He's a keeper."

Lilly lifted her tea glass to her lips and ended the conversation. Somehow, though, her eyes drifted toward the corral where Ian worked with a yearling colt. As if he sensed her watching, he turned, and even though he was too far away for her to see, Lilly knew that he probably winked.

"For someone who doesn't care, you sure melt when you look his way. If you want to fool everyone, you might try working on that lovesick expression on your face. Maybe glare at him from time to time," Jamie teased.

Lilly laughed. "I've missed you, Jamie."

"I've missed you too."

And after that they switched to more neutral topics of conversation. Over the years a lot had happened in their community. Lilly relaxed and pushed away thoughts of Missy, Carl and the one proposal of her life—the one she had turned down.

"Shelby fell and cut her knee." Kathy met them when they pulled into the garage. Lilly jumped from the truck before Ian could cut the engine. He followed her into the house, where Shelby was sitting at the dining room table, tears flowing down her cheeks.

Lilly kneeled next to her, reaching for the blood-soaked washcloth that the little girl held on the cut. Ian watched, knowing that this could be the end of his secret. He almost hoped.

"Let me see, sweetie," Lilly spoke softly to her niece, a tender smile on her lips.

Shelby shook her head no. Her eyes were squeezed shut, and her nose scrunched up.

"I have to see it to know how bad it is." Lilly reached again for the washcloth. Shelby's tears fell harder.

Ian moved forward, ignoring Kathy's hand that tried to restrain him. He kissed the top of Shelby's head and then kneeled next to her.

"You're such a big girl, Shelby. I've seen boys cry harder than you're crying. How'd you get to be so tough? I bet Lilly thinks you're tougher than me." He reached into his pocket and pulled out a pack of gum.

"I'll trade you, a pack of gum for a peek at your knee."

She nodded and took the gum. Lilly mumbled something about cheating. Of course he cheated. He knew what made a kid happy. Gum always did the trick.

He moved the washcloth and gently touched the torn flesh of the child's knee. Not as bad as he had feared.

"I think she needs . . ." Lilly was going to say "stitches." He knew she was, and he stopped her with a curt shake of his head.

"I don't think so, Lil."

"I'm a nurse, Ian."

"And I'm a . . ." He heard Kathy clucking as she moved into the kitchen. She opened the cabinet and he could hear her digging around in search of the first-aid kit that she kept there.

"A what?" Lilly wasn't paying attention to Kathy. Instead she was waiting for him to finish what he had started to say.

"I'm not stupid, Lilly." He heard Kathy mumble something about understatement. He needed to send that woman on another vacation before she got him into serious trouble.

"Ian, I really think that she needs . . . you know."

Shelby started to cry again. "I don't want . . . *you know.*"

Ian chuckled and reached to muss her blond curls. "Don't worry, sweetie, you don't need . . . *you know.* You just need a very good bandage, and I happen to have one."

Kathy had returned and she handed him a first-aid kit. He flipped the lid open and pulled out a butterfly bandage and antibiotic ointment.

"I really think . . ." Lilly continued.

He'd forgotten how she liked to argue. He usually wouldn't have minded, but he wasn't in the mood to argue. His shoulder hurt and that colt back at Jamie's had kicked his shin.

"I'll make you a deal." He glanced up at Lilly as he pulled on gloves and opened the lid to the ointment. "You let me do this and if you still think it needs stitches, we'll take her. But for now, we'll try it my way." He glanced at his watch. "And I need to leave in a few minutes."

Kathy glanced at the clock and then back in his direction. "Do you want me to call and let them know you'll be a little late?"

Ian shook his head in answer, as he squeezed ointment on the cut. The bleeding had already slowed to almost nothing. He opened a butterfly bandage, ignoring the skeptical look that Lilly continued to give him.

"There you go, sweetie." He patted Shelby's arm. "Now, you take it easy for the rest of the night. Stay on the couch, eat a Popsicle and watch cartoons."

"Thank you, *Doctor Ian.*" Lilly shook her head. "You missed your calling."

He winked at her, pulled off the gloves and then gave

Kathy a warning look. "I'm outta here, girls. Kathy, call me if you need me for anything."

Lilly gave him a look, one that clearly said she didn't need him for anything. He let it go. He had a job. He had a life. He needed to let her make her own decisions.

Lilly walked to the window and watched Ian drive away. He constantly amazed her. But then, he'd been doing that since the day she met him. She turned back to the kitchen, where Shelby was sucking away on a cherry Popsicle. Her tears were gone and for now she had forgotten the cut on her leg.

Ian. He had been right about the stitches. Of course, he was used to getting injured. He'd had stitches more than once in his life. He knew what it took.

"What does Ian do at the hospital?" She poured herself a cup of coffee and held the pot out to Kathy.

"Oh, a little of everything." Kathy pulled hamburger out of the freezer and set it in the sink. "Do you two like chili? I thought I'd make some for tomorrow."

"If it isn't too spicy." Lilly leaned against the counter with her cup of coffee and watched a rather guilty-looking Kathy work around the kitchen. The older woman avoided eye contact and pretended the spices in the cabinet were the most interesting things in the world.

"You're not going to tell me."

"About how spicy the chili is? Oh, I don't make it spicy. Johnny can't handle it. Ian says he needs to get that ulcer . . ." She reached into the cabinet and pulled out a jar of chili powder. "Well, anyway, it has to be mild."

"Kathy . . ."

"No, Lilly, I'm not getting into this with you." She set a pan on the stove. "You misunderstand him, and you need to give him a chance, and that's all I'm saying."

Lilly understood quite well. She recognized the mother-bear look on Kathy's face, had seen it more than once. And Lilly knew when to let things go, and when to learn the facts on her own.

All was quiet on the third floor of the hospital. Ian breathed a sigh of relief as he walked down the hall to his office. He slipped inside the darkened room, flipped on a lamp and eased into his chair. The soft leather welcomed him and he sighed as he put his feet up on the desk.

The knock on the door took him by surprise. He had made his rounds, checked on a few patients; as far as everyone knew, he'd left for the night. Obviously someone knew he was still there.

"Come in?" He put his feet down and sat up.

The door opened a crack and a dark head peeked in. Ian felt his heart lurch at the sight of her in this place, and with that hurt, angry look on her face.

She stepped into his office, no smile in sight, and her hands shoved into her pockets.

"I have to give it to you, Dr. Hunt, you're a hard man to nail down."

She walked into the room, stopping in front of his diplomas. She touched the frames, straightening one that tilted to the left.

"Lilly, sit down and I'll get us a cup of coffee."

"I don't want coffee." She turned, still unsmiling, still shooting daggers from her eyes. "I'm not even sure if I want explanations."

"Of course you do. You wouldn't be here if you didn't want to know the truth."

Another rap on the door. Ian groaned, brushed his hand

through his hair and told whoever it was to join the party.

Nurse Anne peeked into the room, "Oh, she found you. I . . ." Anne touched her lip and clicked her tongue a few times. "I guess everything is okay in here?"

"We're just fine, Anne. Thank you."

Lilly watched the door close and then she turned to face Ian. He didn't look any different, but something had changed. Because of what she'd now learned, he was no longer the person she had known.

When Kathy had refused to give her answers, Lilly had asked her to watch Shelby and she'd come to the hospital looking for Ian Hunt. She'd been directed to his office on the pediatric floor.

She watched as he stood up and walked to the coffee pot. He poured two cups, and returned to set them on his desk.

"Have a seat."

She sat down across from him, unable to take her eyes from his face. She continued to see the seventeen-year-old boy who skipped classes and wanted to be a bull rider. Where had this other man come from, the one who looked so in charge, so in control?

The hospital setting was familiar to her. Ian in a white lab coat, sitting behind this wide mahogany desk—that was the thing that was out of place. It didn't fit. And then again, it did.

"I guess you have some 'splaining to do, Lucy." She sipped the coffee. It was too strong and had been on the hot plate too long. Ian didn't seem to notice. Doctors usually didn't; they just wanted the shot of caffeine to keep them awake.

"I guess I do. And I should have done it sooner. I started to the other night, and then you were mad and I didn't have a chance."

"Now you have the chance." Anger, hurt, betrayal . . . she didn't know which emotion to deal with at the moment.

He sipped the coffee and stared at his diplomas. Lilly almost felt sorry for him. Almost.

"When I came here for my senior year, I had already finished two years of college."

"Smart guy, huh?" She switched to humor, hoping to deflect her hurt feelings. They had shared so many secrets as kids.

He had kept this secret from her.

"I came here looking for normal." He leaned back in his chair and stared up at the ceiling. "I had spent time on the farm with Gramps, and I knew that if I came here, I could be a normal teenager. I wanted to have a real senior year. I wanted to hang out with you, spend time on the farm, and relax. I wanted to be my own person, not the person my parents wanted me to be."

"You could have told me."

"No, I couldn't. If I had told you, you wouldn't have treated me the same. I sort of liked it when you worried about my future, and how often I skipped school."

"Creep." She didn't mean it, and he knew it. She had to say something and she didn't know what to say at that moment.

"You still love me." His half-grin didn't look as confident as it normally did.

"No, I don't." She took another sip of the coffee. "And you need to learn to make coffee."

"So, you're going to forgive me?"

"I forgive you, Ian. But this isn't something I can digest all at once. I've known you as one person. Now I'm finding out you're someone completely different. That's going to take time to deal with."

Ian rubbed his hands over his face. When he looked at her she saw how tired he was. She felt a stab of compassion that she didn't want to feel, not at the moment.

"I don't want this to cause problems between us."

"It won't come between us, Ian."

"So you say. You act like I'm a friend, and then you push me away. I never know where I stand with you."

"I'm sorry, Ian. I know that it isn't fair." She didn't know how to explain the fact that he could be a friend, but she feared what her heart wanted. What if she gave in to the feelings she'd had for so many years, and then something happened? What if he let her down? Or worse?

"You've always put conditions on our friendship. You want me to fit into a mold. I can't love the farm. I can't be too involved in your life. To be honest, I can't figure out who or what you want me to be."

"Be who you need to be." She emptied the cup of coffee. "And let me be who I need to be."

If only she knew who she wanted to be. For the last few years she had felt comfortable in her own skin. She had achieved her dreams. She had survived and succeeded. Now she felt as if she was right back where she started. And it had been her choice to come here.

For Shelby. She could do it for her niece. She could live here and give a little girl a chance at a life that included safety and people who would love her.

Music spurted from her purse. Her cell phone. This late in the evening. With a trembling hand she reached for it. The music stopped when she flipped it open and held it to her ear.

"Hello?"

"I can't believe you left Shelby with the old couple. Do you trust me that much?" Carl's sneering voice sent a shiver of fear up her spine. Lilly gripped the phone against her ear.

"Carl, why don't you just leave us alone?" She closed her eyes, heard Ian's chair move, and knew that he was at her side, even before he touched her hand.

"I will, someday. For now, I want you to know what it's like to think you might lose something you want. You took my family from me. You turned my wife against me. I'm going to make you regret that, Lilly. But first I want to see *you* scared, jumping every time *you* hear a noise."

"The police will get you, Carl."

"What police? You mean that friend of yours. That's a joke."

"He'll get you, Carl."

"I'll get you first."

Ian took the phone from her hand, "Listen . . ."

He slammed the phone down on the desk.

"What?" Lilly brushed at her eyes. No tears. Of course there weren't. She had promised herself she wouldn't let Carl break her down.

"He was gone."

"I have to go home and check on Shelby. I have to make sure she's okay." She grabbed her purse and stood up.

"I'm going with you."

"I can take care of myself." She didn't feel so sure about her words, and a part of her was glad he had offered.

"Lilly, I'm off duty. I was heading home anyway."

She nodded, and headed toward the door with Ian behind her. She wasn't alone, and she didn't mind.

Shelby never stirred when they walked into the bedroom. Lilly leaned and kissed the child's cheek before stepping quietly from the room. Ian stood at the door, waiting for her. She ignored the look in his eyes that said he would hurt anyone who tried to hurt her.

She remembered back to another time when that protective look had flashed in his eyes. He had always been this person, out to rescue, to save the world. And she had always been fighting him, determined to save herself.

She should have been able to rely on her parents. They hadn't meant to, but they had always let her down. Her mother had been too hurt by life. Her father had never been able to accept the responsibilities of adulthood.

That had left Lilly to take up the slack.

"You're safe here." Ian's quiet words, so sure, so determined, brought her out of the distant past and back to the present.

"I'm trying to believe that." She followed him down the stairs and into the kitchen. "Sit down and I'll fix you something to eat."

Ian's brows arched and he shook his head. "I can get it, you sit down. You have to learn that it isn't always necessary for you to take care of everyone."

"I have to take care of my family." She sat on one of the stools at the island.

"Okay, fine, I can handle that. But every now and then, let a friend do something for you. No strings attached."

No strings. She knew that he would keep his word. He had kept it all those years ago when he'd come home from college for her mother's funeral. He had known her need to get away, to start over. He'd paid for her mother's funeral and then given her the money to leave. Over the years she had sent money orders to pay him back. He had never tried to track her down.

Sometimes that hurt. A silly female part of her had wondered why he hadn't tried to find her. It would have been easy to do. Another part of her knew that he was keeping his promise to let her go, and she admired him for that.

"Do you want anything to eat?" His question nudged her from thoughts that were dangerous.

"No, I'm fine."

He took his plate out of the microwave and sat down next to her. "So, what are we going to do about Carl?"

"There is no *we*." She sighed. "Okay, I guess there is. You're always there, pulling me out of hot water."

"And you're always fighting, telling me that you can take care of yourself. You remind me of a wild kitten that needs a warm barn and a bowl of milk, but you're too busy scratching me to realize that I'm trying to help."

"Cute analogy. So now I'm a mangy, flea-bitten cat. Just what every woman wants to be. So, if you ever call me kitten . . ."

Ian laughed, and Lilly couldn't stop herself from joining him. It felt good to find humor in a moment that seemed dark. Somehow, with Ian sitting next to her, life didn't seem hopeless.

She had her own faith, but his was stronger ,and maybe it was as contagious as his laughter.

"Remember when you asked me to marry you?" She knew that he did. How could he have forgotten?

"I still have the emotional scars. You wanted out of here, and this life. You made it pretty clear that marrying me would resign you to the life your mother had led."

"I want to apologize for that."

"Things aren't always what they seem?" He laughed, but more softly, and not with the same humor as earlier.

"No, and after all that you had done for me, I shouldn't have been that way, not to you."

"Thank you, I think." He finished a bite of chili before speaking again. "Does that mean you would have given my proposal more consideration? Now that you know the truth?"

"No, I don't think so. We were kids, and friends. We weren't in love."

He didn't answer right away. Lilly glanced at him. The look on his face made her wonder what she had missed.

"You're right," he finally answered. "We couldn't have built a marriage on anything that basic. Well, I need to get to bed. I have a long day at the office tomorrow."

"Good night, Ian."

He offered her his customary half-grin and a wink before he stood up and walked away. He had left his bowl and glass. Lilly picked them up and carried them to the dishwasher, but her mind was far away, on leftover feelings from long ago.

Her heart forced her to remember how a kiss had felt. Of course she couldn't listen to her heart. It had never understood that Ian wasn't the right one for her. He was a cowboy. Cowboys didn't make good husbands and fathers. She knew that from experience.

Her heart tried to convince her that some cowboys did make good husbands. She thought about Johnny, who was nothing like her father. And obviously Ian wasn't either.

Lilly couldn't concentrate on the book she had brought with her to the park. Her gaze would leave the words, searching for Shelby in the group of children on the play equipment.

The moment they had arrived the other children had pulled Shelby into their play. These kids weren't aware of what Missy had done. These kids weren't going to tease Lilly's niece about her mother. They didn't know that Missy was in prison.

"Hey."

Lilly jumped, even though the voice was familiar. She closed the book and smiled up at Ian. He sat down next to her.

"What are you doing here?" She hadn't meant for it to come out that way. "I'm sorry, I'm just surprised to see you."

"It's four o'clock and I'm done for the day. I called home before I left the office and Kathy said you were at the park. So, what were you thinking about when I walked up? You looked like you were a million miles away."

"I was thinking about Missy, and about Kansas City. This is why I came home, to give Shelby moments like this."

"You couldn't find moments like this in Kansas City?"

She shrugged and considered his question. "I think we might have, but I was tired of the rat race. I knew that Shelby was being teased at preschool. Can you believe that? Preschool children picking on her because of what her mother had done."

"Kids learn a lot from their parents."

"True. And then there was a situation at a park in our neighborhood. I never took Shelby there, but just two months ago the police made a drug bust there after a child came home with needles she had found near the swings."

Ian didn't respond, but she didn't really need to hear his opinion. What he felt was written on his face, in the grim line of his mouth, and the narrowing of his eyes as he watched the group of children play.

"Childhood should be a happy time." He spoke quietly, and in a tone that made her wonder if his childhood had been happy.

Someday she might ask him. Not today. Not only because she wasn't ready, but from the look on his face, he didn't seem to be ready to tell everything about his life.

"I just want her to be safe. To have a childhood free from teasing. I don't want her to be judged for what her parents have done."

Lilly felt an ache in the region of her heart as she said those words. Too many times in her childhood she had lived through the nightmare of being her father's daughter. In school, at family gatherings, and sometimes even in church. People could be cruel, and forget that children were sometimes innocent victims of their upbringing.

She wanted Shelby to have better.

"You can't protect her from everything." Ian sighed. "But it would be nice if you could."

Lilly's phone jangled with music she really needed to change. She reached into her purse, almost afraid to answer. When she said, "Hello," it was the automated voice of an operator asking if she would accept a collect call from Missy. Lilly answered, "Yes," and then she waited for the call to connect.

"Lilly." Missy's voice, questioning, and timid. What had happened to the girl who had wanted to conquer the world?

"Missy, how are you?"

"I'm better. Lilly, I have to tell you something." A long pause, and Lilly felt her heart racing as she imagined the things her sister might say. "Last night I remembered something. I remembered that I did tell Carl about the farm. It was a long time ago. Maybe he's forgotten where it is."

A momentary flash of anger with her sister startled Lilly. Eyes closed, she fought for patience that seemed to be in short supply, but somehow she found a small reserve. Missy had her own share of guilt without Lilly adding to it.

"I'm glad you told me. Don't worry, we'll be safe."

"You won't, Lilly. Not as long as Carl is out there."

"Don't worry." Lilly had that covered. She could worry enough for all of them.

"I have to worry. I don't want him to hurt you or Shelby."

"I won't let him." Lilly almost sighed as the words weighed down on her. "I'll keep Shelby safe."

"I know you will," Missy sobbed. "I have to go."

And then the phone clicked and went dead.

Ian's hand was on her arm, strong and comforting. At that moment it would have been easy to let him take over. Lilly took a deep breath and told herself she could handle this.

She remembered a verse from her Sunday school lesson a few months earlier. Because of her schedule she hadn't always been able to get to church. But some lessons stuck with a person.

He who dwelleth in the secret place of the Most High, shall abide under the shadow of the Almighty. And I will say of the Lord, He is my refuge and fortress, my God in Him shall I trust.

She could trust God to keep them safe. She had to believe that. She had to be strong and stand on her faith.

"Lilly, I'm here if you need anything. Or if you want to talk."

"I know. I don't know that there is anything to say. Carl is playing a cat-and-mouse game with us, and in the end he plans to win. I'm not going to let him."

"You're not alone."

She smiled at him, "Thank you." But there was something more, something she had remembered from Carl's phone call.

"Ian, there's something Carl said. I didn't think about it too much at the time, but now I'm just not sure what it means."

Ian leaned toward her, his earnest gaze searching. "What?"

"He knows about Dean being at the farm. How does he know that?"

Ian leaned back, his left ankle crossed over his right knee. The lines around his mouth tensed and he shook his head. Lilly waited, hoping he had answers.

"A scanner."

"What?"

Ian looked at her. "He has a scanner. He knows when the police have been called. He listens to them talking to each other."

Lilly shivered in the warm sunshine. "We're not going to be able to stop him."

"Yes, we'll stop him. We're smarter and there are more of us."

Lilly sighed, "I hope you're right."

The house lay in quiet darkness. Ian tread silently across the great room, trying hard not to sound like a herd of cattle stampeding . . . as Kathy often accused him of. He had been home from work for an hour, had eaten leftovers, and now wanted nothing more than a hot shower and a good night's sleep.

Headlights flashed across the log walls of the room. Unusual for that time of night on a quiet country road. He listened to the rattle of an older car engine as it idled to a stop. He changed course and moved across the room to the window. The car was 200 feet from his drive, the headlights now turned off.

"Who is it?" a voice whispered from behind him, making him jump. That hurt his pride a little, jumping in the night like a frightened child. Brave men don't jump.

"I'm not sure, and don't sneak up behind a guy."

"I didn't mean to scare you," Lilly whispered.

"I wasn't scared," he protested, keeping his eyes on the car. He pointed to the phone. "Call nine-one-one."

Lilly reached for the cordless phone. "What if it's just a person with car problems?"

"At midnight on this road?" He took the phone away from her and dialed.

"Nine-one-one, do you have an emergency?" the operator's voice answered, seeming loud in the stillness of the night.

"Yes, I do. A prowler in a car outside of my house. We think it might be someone we know . . ." He looked at Lilly. "What is Carl's last name?"

"Carl Long."

"Carl Long. He's wanted in Kansas City for manufacturing meth. And also, you might need to know that we think he has a scanner."

"I'll send a car right out."

The dispatcher took more information and hung up.

Ian wrapped an arm around Lilly and felt her tremble beneath his hand. He pulled her closer to his side. "We'll get him, Lil."

"Will we?"

"Of course." He hugged her and then let her go. "I want you to stay in here. When I go out the front door, you lock it, and you don't open it again until I tell you. And if Dean calls, let him know that I'm not letting this guy get away. Oh, and tell him about the scanner."

"You can't be serious! You're not going after him." She bit down on her lip as she shoved her hands into her pockets, a stormy look brewing on her darkened face. "I won't let you."

The headlights of the car flashed on and the engine spurted back to life. Ian leaned against the corner of the window, hoping to see blue lights flashing in the dark night. In a big county, late at night, sometimes it could take awhile for a deputy to arrive.

"He does have a scanner. He must have heard the call, and our address. I need to go after him. We can't let him get away." He started to move away, but Lilly pulled him back. "Lilly, I have to. He's going to get away." He reached into his pocket for his keys.

"The police will get him."

"They can't get here soon enough."

"Ian, don't leave. What if he's doing this to get you to chase him, and then he'll come back and we'll be alone."

Her voice trembled, and in the moonlit room her face paled. Ian sighed. He watched as the car sped away, accompanied by the hiccupping sound of an engine on its last legs. Maybe, with any help from above, the car would break down and the police would find him on the side of the road.

"I'm not going anywhere." He pulled her to him and held her close.

At the moment he couldn't do anything about the taillights that rounded a curve and disappeared from view. He couldn't leave Lilly and Shelby, knowing that Carl might come back.

Lilly held on to Ian, not willing to let him go, even if letting go meant capturing Carl. She couldn't be alone. She felt suddenly weak, unable to stand on her own. Maybe she wasn't strong at all. And that thought frightened her. Her mother hadn't been a strong woman.

Ian's hand touched the back of her head, stroking her hair, calming her with his touch. He gentled horses the same way. She'd watched him do it—take a wild foal and turn it into a docile pet that followed him around the corral.

"This will all work out, Lilly. They'll catch him, and things will return to normal."

She nodded against his shirt and then she realized that she'd been in his arms for a long time. She needed to put distance between them, and between her heart and his.

"Life was so good, Ian." She brushed her hair back from her face. "Things were going right for me. Sometimes I feel like I can't catch a break."

"Life is about change, Lilly. Things happen and shake us out of our plans, out of the path we decide for ourselves. This is just one of those things, but it won't last forever. Hard times cycle around, followed by good times. Don't let this drag you down."

"I know." She leaned her cheek against the window, staring out into the inky black night, now devoid of headlights.

A few minutes later, blue lights flashed in the darkness, and headlights appeared over the top of the hill.

"I think I should leave." She didn't look at him, but knew that the words would make him angry.

"You mean you think you should run? And when he finds you? What then?"

"Run again." She couldn't meet his eyes.

"Stay and fight, Lilly." He moved toward the door, not waiting for her. "And after we catch Carl, then, if you want, you can leave."

He made it sound so easy.

CHAPTER 8

The aroma of baking chicken greeted Ian as he walked into the house from the barn. He kicked off his boots and headed to the sink to wash his hands.

"Where's Lilly?" he asked Kathy as she walked in from the utility room.

"She's down at her place."

Her place. Ian rinsed his hand and reached for a paper towel. He ripped one off, dried his hands, taking a moment to think about Lilly and her determination to make the house down the road her home again.

"What's she doing down there?"

Kathy ignored his question.

"Kathy?"

"She's having a security system installed, and some furniture delivered." She opened the cabinet below the sink and pulled out some cleaning supplies.

"Security system? She didn't tell me she was going to do that." He avoided making eye contact with Kathy, knowing she would give him that knowing look of hers. "Okay, it was my idea, but I thought we'd talk about it before she moved forward."

"She's a big girl, Ian, and she likes to take care of herself."

"Of course." He dropped the damp paper towel into the trash. "I think a security system is a good idea."

Kathy laughed. "I admire the restraint you're showing. I know how you'd like to run down there and take over.

Letting her do this on her own is the best move you can make."

Ian had to smile, "You know me too well. And you're right. She needs space. But I did want to invite her to the rodeo tonight."

"Then invite her, but don't be surprised if she says no. And don't go running down to her place right now."

Good advice. Ian begrudgingly admitted that Kathy had a point. Lilly wouldn't thank him for interfering in this. He could invite her to the rodeo later.

"I hate rodeos. I can't believe I let you talk me into this." Lilly wiggled her fingers loose from Ian's hand as they crossed the grassy expanse between the parking area full of trucks and trailers and the arena. Crowds milled, people drank sodas, kids ate cotton candy. It looked festive. It looked like a wonderful family evening. It had never been that for her.

"Stop thinking about the past." Ian took her hand in his; this time she didn't free herself. "Look at Shelby. She's seeing it as a wonderful, magical night."

"She doesn't have to count on this for food on the table."

"No, she doesn't. And neither do you, not now."

She had to give him that. And Shelby was having the time of her young life. In her childhood there had been a few times when this life had been entertainment. She could remember being Shelby's age, and the pride she had felt as she watched her dad ride a bull for the full eight seconds.

On her sixteenth birthday Ian had taken her to the rodeo in Tulsa. They had made a day of it, and he had even taken her out to dinner. She had felt so grown up and he had made her feel so special. Good memories that she had kept buried like treasure in her heart.

"Promise me you won't get hurt," she whispered, chancing a glance in his direction.

"Cross my heart."

She wanted to believe him.

"I want to be a rodeo girl when I grow up." Shelby had squirmed between them and now held each of their hands, jumping and bouncing as they walked, and sometimes lifting her feet to swing between them.

"No!" Lilly startled herself with the outburst. She eased out a smile to soften the word. "No, you don't want to be a rodeo girl. You want to be something like a doctor, or maybe a teacher."

"You could be a barrel racer," Ian offered.

Lilly gave him a look that he couldn't misinterpret. His interference wasn't welcomed in this matter. Something about the smile he shot her way told her he didn't care.

"Yes, yes, a barrel racer." Shelby let go of their hands, raced off and then back to them, pretending to be on a horse.

"Don't do this, Ian."

"She's a little girl who wants to dream of horses, Lilly. That isn't unusual, so let her dream."

Lilly sighed. "Yes, you're right."

Shelby ran back to them and Ian picked her up and swung her in the air. "Do you want to ride a barrel horse?"

Outnumbered, Lilly gave up. Ian had Shelby on his shoulders and they were heading toward a horse tied to a horse trailer. A tall, leggy blonde was cinching up the saddle on the gold-coated palomino. A jab of jealousy stabbed at Lilly's gut, which wasn't fair or right.

"Hey, Connie."

The blonde turned and bestowed a gorgeous smile on Ian.

"Ian, I wasn't sure if you'd be here after that fall. How are things at the hospital?"

"You can't keep a good man down."

"I've heard that before." *Blond and beautiful* patted the neck of her horse. "Are you going to ride tonight?"

"I plan on it." He picked up Shelby. "I was wondering if you would help out a future barrel racer. This is Shelby and she would love to ride a real barrel horse."

"Of course she can ride Jack. I was just going to warm him up out in the field. She can ride him first, before he realizes he's working tonight."

Lilly remained silent, wondering who Connie was to Ian. Not that it mattered. She could have stopped him from putting her niece on the horse. She decided to let it go. Shelby didn't have to grow up resenting horses, and the rodeo. Lilly was the one with the memories of grocery money going toward the purchase of another horse, or fees for a rodeo, or sometimes being gambled on the outcome of a ride.

Shelby saw only a tall, noble animal with trusting brown eyes.

And the delight on Shelby's face as Connie led her around the grassy lot at the back of the rodeo grounds made it worth Lilly's own discomfort. She wouldn't have taken that moment away from her niece for anything. Shelby deserved to dream of horses and happier times.

Shelby rode the horse as if she'd been riding her whole life. And she beamed with true happiness as the horse broke into a slow trot. Lilly hugged herself as she watched the little girl that had become hers only because of the wrong choices her parents had made.

Not for the first time Lilly realized the magnitude of the responsibility she had taken when the judge proclaimed her

Shelby's legal guardian. Shelby was hers. She was responsible not only for keeping her safe, but for loving her, for giving her a happy home, for providing her with good memories.

"Chin up, Lilly, it'll all work out." Ian moved closer, his arm brushing hers. "You're home, and we're all going to be here for you."

"I know that, Ian. I guess I'm still coming to terms with the reality that I'm more than Shelby's aunt. I need to be her mother."

"You're a good mother to her. Don't worry, you are being what she needs."

Lilly nodded but she couldn't answer. A lump the size of Texas had formed in her throat. When the horse with its happy rider trotted back in their direction, Lilly managed to smile.

"I want a horse just like this one, Aunt Lilly."

"Maybe you can have one when you're a little bigger," Lilly promised, and the promise hurt.

She remembered back to the years when she had wanted a pony. That had been so long ago and the desire for a horse hadn't lasted for her.

"I have to get ready. Are you going to be okay?" Ian's hand was on her arm. She smiled up at him.

"Yeah, I'm going to be okay. But please be careful."

He tipped his hat and winked. Why did he have to do that? Why did he have to be handsome and charming? Why did he have to attach strings that he didn't even know he was attaching? Strings that felt like they were connecting her heart to his.

Nothing a good pair of scissors wouldn't cure.

Ian lowered himself onto the bull's broad back. The

huge brown beast snorted and tried to climb out of the chute. It shook its head and white foam flew out at them.

Adrenaline shot through him like a drug, making his heart race. He tensed, his body preparing for the moment when the gate would open. With the rope wrapped around his hand, head down, knees steady against the heaving sides of the beast, he nodded and the gate flew open.

The bull jumped from the chute, spinning to the right as it unleashed a ton of fury in an effort to rid itself of the rider on its back. Ian fell forward, jerked to the side, left hand up, shoulder screaming in protest.

He breathed in the dirty sweat of the beast and felt the animal hunch and lurch to one side. Somehow he stayed on its back, even with the pain in his shoulder screaming for him to jump.

As the buzzer rang, ending the eight-second ride, he unwound the rope from his hand and jumped, rolling away from the snorting animal as it turned and moved toward him, ready to toss him into the air or pound him into the dirt of the arena.

A flash of blue and white flew between Ian and the bull. A bullfighter, ready to take the brunt of the bull's attack. Ian took advantage of the animal's momentary distraction, jumped to his feet and ran for the fence. He jumped, swinging himself over a panel just as the bull charged again, horns clanging against the metal of the gate.

The roar of the crowd, the snort of the bull, the smell of sweat and dirt, all mingled in an overload of sensation. Ian watched the bull running out of the pen and then he jumped down, bowed to the crowd and limped out of the arena.

"You okay, Doc?" One of the bullfighters, responsible for keeping the riders safe from charging bulls, slapped him on the back as he walked past him.

Ian cringed as the innocent touch jarred his shoulder.

"Doing great, Ken. Thanks a lot for saving my skin out there."

Ken laughed. "Seems I saved more than your skin."

"Ian."

He looked back and saw that it was Lilly calling his name, and Shelby ran alongside her. He smiled good-bye to Ken and headed in their direction.

"Ninety points, now that's a ride." He tugged on Shelby's blond curls.

"I'm so happy for you." Lilly didn't sound happy. He tipped his hat back and gave her a look. The frown she returned was answer enough. Nope, she wasn't happy.

"I promise you this, Lilly, this is my last year riding bulls."

"Don't make promises to me. I'm not your keeper."

"Fine, you're not my keeper."

Just the keeper of his heart. That sounded too poetical for someone who was supposed to be a cowboy, so he kept the thought safely tucked away for a better day. Those words fit a romantic, candlelit dinner. And even then, he didn't know how well received the words would be. He had a feeling getting stomped on by a rowdy bull would hurt less than having his heart stomped on by Lilly.

"I'm ready to go home." That came from Shelby.

Ian looked down at the little girl. She definitely looked ready to go home. She was pale and her eyes were rimmed with red. He put a hand to her forehead.

"She's running a fever." He squatted in front of her, his leg muscles protesting the movement. "Where do you feel bad, sweetheart?"

"My stomach." And then she burst into tears.

"Probably all of that cotton candy you bought her." Lilly picked the child up and kissed her forehead. "But she does feel warm."

"I don't feel good, Aunt Lilly."

"Of course you don't. We'll take you home and put you to bed."

Ian forgot his shoulder, and even the pull in his left leg. He reached for Shelby and Lilly handed her to him. They headed across the parking lot, their big night over, Shelby crying softly against his shoulder.

"How is Shelby?" Ian leaned the pitchfork against the side of the stall he was cleaning and pulled off his gloves as he walked out to greet Lilly.

"She's fine, I think. She was sick a few times during the night, but this morning she's up and having waffles for breakfast."

"Good, I'm glad to hear that." He waited, wondering what she would say. He watched as she looked around the barn, and he knew that she was remembering. How could she forget?

"You kissed me for the first time in this barn." Her smile softened as she looked around.

"Yes, I guess I did."

How could he forget? She had walked down the road, barefoot in cutoff jeans and a T-shirt. But he hadn't really been paying attention to how she looked. The tears and the red handprint on her cheek had been on his mind that day. Her dad, in a drunken rage, had slapped her.

"You've always been here to rescue me." She leaned against the door to a stall and looked in at the mare. "She's beautiful."

"Thank you." He leaned next to her. "I've always considered you a friend, and friends do that for each other."

"I know." She smiled at him. "And even though I haven't acted like one, I consider you a friend, too. And I think I've neglected thanking you for all that you did."

"Any friend would have done the same."

She shook her head. "No, Ian, that isn't true. You came home from college when Mom died. You used your own money to give Missy and me a new start."

"You deserved that chance."

"I don't know why you think that." The mare stepped close and Lilly rubbed the gray muzzle that nibbled at her arm.

"Because you did, Lilly. I don't want to argue about this. You worked so hard and gave up so much to help your family. I wanted to make things easier for you."

"I feel like I owe you."

"You paid me back." He leaned against her, shoulder to shoulder. "I only ask that you stop trying to act like I'm the enemy. Let me keep you safe and when all of this is over, you can do whatever you feel you need to do."

"I hate that you're taking off from work." She hadn't believed him when he told her of the decision the previous night. He called it a vacation that he'd been putting off. She knew that it was because of her. "They probably need you there. And I do need to get the house ready to move into."

"They're fine without me and they know that they can call if they really do need me. Don't worry, a retired friend is taking my patients. I'm still going into the hospital. The time off will probably be good for me. And I can help you with the house."

"Why did you always act like school didn't matter?"

He had known it would only be a matter of time before she went back to that old topic. He moved away from the stall, away from the woman who stood there, watching him. He shoved his hands back into his gloves and grabbed the pitchfork.

"My life had been about education since I turned three. I needed a break. I needed time away from a group of friends who were pulling me in the wrong direction." He tried to smile, but this time the gesture didn't come as easily.

"I guess I never really knew you, did I?"

"You knew me, Lil. You just didn't know everything you thought you knew."

The sound of car tires crunching against the gravel drive that led to the barn caught his attention. Ian glanced in Lilly's direction. Her mouth had tightened into a grim line and she moved toward him.

"Don't worry, it's probably nobody." Ian walked away from her. "Stay here until I see."

A long and very out-of-place sedan pulled up to the barn. The driver looked like anything but a drug dealer. Of course looks could be deceiving, and Ian didn't feel like dropping his guard—instead he felt territorial, like the hair on the back of his neck should be rising in warning.

Lilly groaned and mumbled something he couldn't understand.

"I take it that isn't Carl?"

"No, that's not Carl." She shoved her hands into her back pockets. "That's Dan."

"And Dan would be?" More bristling as he recognized the other man as competition.

"A friend of mine from Kansas City."

Her explanation didn't satisfy Ian. "A boyfriend?"

"No, not a boyfriend, just a friend. He's worried about me."

"How nice." Ian turned when he heard the back door to the barn close with a thud. Johnny had been in the corral feeding the stallion. The older man headed in their direction, his gait slower than it had been years ago when Ian first came here.

Ian turned to watch his uninvited guest get out of the sedan. Lilly moved away from his side, toward the other man. Friend? Or something more? Ian watched the two approach one another and he fought off the need to follow, to involve himself in their conversation.

"Dan."

"Lilly, I just wanted to see for myself that you're okay." The guy stepped carefully, avoiding the certain pitfalls that came with farm living, and driving a luxury car up to a barn.

"I'm fine. I'm tired, but I'm okay," Lilly told him as he leaned on the hood of his car and looked at the bottom of his shoe.

Ian stepped back into the barn. He didn't want to see more. Johnny followed him as he headed to the next stall that he needed to clean.

"You just gonna leave 'em out there together?" Johnny pushed the wheelbarrow up to the stall.

"I reckon I am." He pitched old straw out of the stall. "She's a big girl, Johnny."

"Yes, she is." The older man shook his head. "And you're about to goof up."

"She has to make her own decisions." Even if it hurts.

He had almost finished cleaning the last stall when she returned. Ian waited, wondering what she would say. If she had decided to go back to Kansas City, he wouldn't try to stop her.

"Can you keep an eye on Shelby for an hour? Dan wants to

take me out for lunch before he heads back to Kansas City."

Ian shrugged. "Sure, I can watch her. Take your cell phone in case we need to get hold of you."

She stood on tiptoes and kissed his cheek. "Thank you."

He watched her leave, knowing that Johnny stood behind him, waiting to make some kind of comment. As the car pulled away, the older man proved him right.

"Well, there she goes, and you just stood there and watched her leave." He shook his head and mumbled something about leading a horse to water, which didn't make sense to Ian.

"Leave matchmaking to the women, Johnny." He walked into the stable office and grabbed a cola out of the fridge. He handed a bottle of water to his foreman. "I'm going to head to the house for a sandwich. Are you coming with me?"

"I'll be up in a few minutes. I want to put the mare and foal back into the corral."

"Stay out of the caffeine," Ian warned as he walked away. He glanced over his shoulder in time to see Johnny heading back into the office with the unopened bottle of water.

Kathy met Ian at the front door. Her brow was wrinkled with worry and she motioned him into the house. He kicked off his boots and followed her up the stairs.

"She's been throwing up for thirty minutes, Ian." She practically pushed him into the upstairs bathroom. "I'm really worried about her."

"Relax, Kathy. She's going to be fine." But on first glance he wasn't so sure of that. Shelby was curled up on the bathroom floor, a blanket around her shoulders. She peeked up at him, her tear-streaked face pale and glistening with perspiration.

"What's up, kiddo?" He kneeled and picked the child up. "Do you think maybe we should check you out and maybe take you to get some medicine?"

She nodded but didn't say anything.

"Can I touch your stomach?"

She shook her head and started to cry again. "It hurts too bad."

"I'm just going to put my fingers on your side." He set her down on the bed and pulled the blanket off her shoulders.

"I want Aunt Lilly." Tears streamed down her cheeks and she started to sob.

"I know, honey. We'll call her and have her meet us at the hospital." He touched her stomach and when his fingers hit the right side of her belly, she flinched and cried again.

"I don't wanna go to a doctor." She rubbed at her eyes and her bottom lip trembled.

"Can I tell you a secret?" He leaned and whispered in her ear. When he did, her tears stopped and her eyes widened. "Now, come on. I'll take you to meet a friend of mine."

CHAPTER 9

Heart pounding, and fear chasing away the voice that told her to be calm, Lilly raced into the waiting area of the emergency room. She had prayed—prayed for Shelby, and for peace. Surely God wouldn't ignore her pleas for a child that they both loved?

He could ignore her on everything else, but she begged Him not to ignore this one prayer. Somewhere in there she thought about making a deal, but her conscience got the better of her. God didn't need her promises, or her bargains. He needed her time, and her prayers. She needed faith.

She spotted Johnny and Kathy, and hurried to where they were sitting.

"Where is she?" Breathless from running, the words came out sounding harsh. She closed her eyes and took a deep breath. "I'm sorry, I didn't mean to snap."

"She's in the examining room with Ian. It's her appendix." Kathy reached for her hand. "She's fine, Lilly. Ian won't let anything happen to her. You go on back."

Lilly nodded and turned away from their concerned looks. A receptionist stopped her at the doors to the ER. "I'm sorry, ma'am, you can't go back there."

"My little girl is back there. Her name is Shelby Long."

"Oh. She's with Dr. Hunt. Come on, I'll show you where they are."

As they reached the last cubicle, the curtain opened and Ian stepped out. It took her a moment to accept that this man, in his white coat, was the same Ian that she knew. With his longish, sun-streaked brown hair, it was easy to picture him in faded jeans and a T-shirt. And yet he seemed at home here, with the jeans and T-shirt covered with a white lab coat and a stethoscope around his neck.

"How is she?" Lilly tried to push past him, but his hand on her arm stopped her.

"Take a deep breath and calm down before you go in there," he warned.

"Don't tell me to calm down. I left her, Ian. I left her and she was sick. Worse than that, what if Carl had been watching, waiting for me to leave."

He pulled her away from the cubicle. His hand on her elbow was firm, refusing to release her when she tried to jerk free from his grasp.

"She needs for you to go in there smiling. She needs for you to be calm. As a nurse, you know that."

"I do know that." She brushed a hand across her face. "But I feel so guilty."

She closed her eyes and took a deep breath. He was right. Her first concern had to be for Shelby. This wasn't about her, or her guilt. "I need to go to her." She opened her eyes. Ian didn't release her arm. "I'm fine now."

"I know you are." His hand dropped to his side. "I wanted you to know that we're going to have to do surgery. We need to get that appendix out."

"Okay, but I want to be with her."

"No."

"Yes."

"No, you won't be with her. We have a very capable staff and neither of us will be babysitting them to see that they do their job."

She released a sigh. "I need to hold her."

"Come on. She's a little sleepy right now, but she could use a hug. And then you'll have to sign a release."

Lilly nodded and walked away from him. As she stepped into the cubicle where her niece was sleeping, she managed to push away her guilt and her fear, to concentrate on the little girl who so desperately needed for her to be strong. She sat on a chair near the bed and reached for the small hand that had short, slim fingers like Missy's.

"Please, God, help her to get well soon." She whispered the prayer, and didn't fight against the tears that squeezed out.

Shelby opened her eyes and smiled a tremulous smile. "Aunt Lilly."

"I'm here, sweetheart. I'm sorry that I left you when you were sick."

"It's okay, Ian's a doctor and he took care of me."

"Yes, Ian's a doctor." She smiled, and brushed the tangle of blond curls back from Shelby's face. "And he knows the people who are going to help you to get better."

"He said he'll make sure I get better soon, so that I can ride my pony."

"Your pony?"

Shelby only nodded and then she drifted off again. The curtain moved and Ian stepped into the room, a guilty flush staining his cheeks. He didn't offer an explanation about the pony. Wordlessly, he sat down on a stool near the bed and folded his hands in his lap—so Ian, and yet so not.

"They're ready to take her up. We can go up to the second-floor waiting room." He rolled the stool to her side and reached for her hands. His fingers, warm and strong, wrapped around hers. "First, we're going to pray."

She bowed her head without answering. His words of faith, so strong and sure, washed over her in peaceful waves. At that moment he believed enough for both of them. She was reassured by that.

It had always been easy to blame God when things went wrong. She shouldn't, she knew that, but sometimes the feelings sneaked up on her, robbing her of the faith she normally tried to stand on, to rely on.

The loss of her father, the years of hunger and never making ends meet, her mother's suicide—a jab of pain accompanied that thought—it had always been easy to question God in those situations. She had believed in Him, and still did, but why did it sometimes seem as though He was so far away?

She looked down at the hand holding hers, and listened to the softly spoken prayer. And she realized that God had never really let her down. People had. And God had sent other people to help, to pick her up when she needed it most.

Even now, there were people in her life who cared and who would help her to get through this. Peace descended, blanketing her in warmth.

Ian said a firm "Amen," squeezed her hand and then he stood up. Lilly looked up, her vision blurring as tears covered the surface of her eyes.

"Thank you, Ian. For everything."

He brushed his hand across her cheek.

"Come on. Kathy and Johnny are already on their way upstairs. The orderly is waiting to take Shelby."

"Make sure they take care of her, Ian."

"Don't worry, they're all the best." He put a hand on her shoulder, comforting, the hand of a doctor. "Kiss her before we go."

Tears streaming down her cheeks, Lilly leaned over to kiss her niece. Concern made it hard to leave. But she was no longer afraid. Ian's prayer had brought her a peace she hadn't expected to feel.

★ ★ ★ ★ ★

"What's taking so long?" Lilly looked up at the clock again. She paced through the waiting room, back to her seat, sat down, and then got up to pace again.

Ian watched, unable to do anything to take away her fear, or her frustration. He felt it too, a small nudge of impatience that he had been fighting for the last thirty minutes of watching the clock tick off one minute after another.

"It hasn't been that long." He walked to her side and put an arm around her waist. "Come and sit down."

"I can't sit down. I want to know what is wrong. I feel it, Ian. I feel like there's something wrong. Please go check."

Her lips were drawn in a tight line and her face was pale. He touched her cheek and she closed her eyes, sooty lashes dipping to shadow her cheeks. The sigh she released was long and full of emotion. The sigh of a worried mother. A child didn't have to be biological to be part of a person.

"I'll go check." He led her back to the chair next to Kathy's. "Sit here and let Kathy pray with you."

He walked out of the waiting room into the brightly lit corridor that smelled of antiseptic and pine cleaner. He loved the smell, had always loved it. Since he turned ten, he had known that he would be a doctor. The dream had come easily. Medical school had been a breeze for him. Being a normal kid had never been that easy.

A nurse met him outside the OR. She had obviously been on her way to update them on Shelby's condition. The worried crease in her brow brought a moment of doubt. He chased it away. After telling Lilly to have faith, he had to remember to keep his own.

"What's up?" He pulled the nurse away from the waiting room where Lilly might overhear.

"There's some infection. We're getting her closed up now,

but it was a little worse than we had originally thought."

Ian slammed the palm of his hand against the wall. "That's my fault. I should have brought her in last night. I thought it was something she ate, and that it would pass."

"It isn't your fault, Dr. Hunt. She's probably been fighting this for several days and just ignored the symptoms. You know how these things go."

He leaned forward, resting his forehead on the cool block wall. Nurse Jennings touched his shoulder. "Nobody will blame you for this. You brought her in and she's going to be fine."

"I should have caught it."

"Ian, get a grip and stop acting like God." The masculine voice belonged to Devon Jacks. Ian stood back, rubbing his hands across his face. He turned to face his friend.

"Yeah, you're right."

"Of course I'm right. And I'm right about the God complex, too. You're not God, and when you try to do His, job, you stink. You're one of the best pediatricians in the country, and you're a man of faith, but you can't see into the future or perform miracles. This little girl is going to be fine."

"Thanks, Jacks. I guess I'll go back and let her aunt know that she's okay."

"Do, and I'll see you around here tomorrow. But don't stay the night. We have a staff of nurses that we pay for that specific reason. They're good and they do a great job of taking care of patients."

Ian grinned. "Nothing like a friend to keep me on the straight and narrow."

"That's what friends are for."

Three pairs of eyes glanced in his direction when he walked into the waiting room. Lilly stood up, her expression expectant. He took her hand in his and sat down. She dropped into the seat next to his.

"What is it?"

"They're finished. There's some infection, not too bad, nothing to cause her any long-term problems. She's going to be fine, but she's going to be here for a few days while they treat her with antibiotics."

Lilly buried her face in her hands and cried. Ian touched her back and waited until her sobs receded. He rubbed gently, wanting so badly to take her in his arms and comfort her, and seek comfort.

"She's fine, Lil."

"I should have known," she whispered into her hands.

Ian reached for the box of tissues on the table next to his chair. He pulled a few out and handed them to her. "I should have known, Lilly."

He leaned back in his chair and closed his eyes. He heard Kathy whispering to Lilly, and heard Lilly's whispered replies. He heard them praying and then heard Johnny's gruff "Amen."

It was Johnny's faith that had been a light in a pretty dark world for Ian. That had been so many years ago, and sometimes it seemed like yesterday. And today. Johnny was still a rock, even now.

"We're going to go on home and feed." Johnny patted his knee and Ian opened his eyes.

"Thanks, Johnny."

"You're welcome, son." Son. Ian smiled his thanks to the older man. "Take care of our girls."

"I will." He took the hand that Kathy held out to him, and when she leaned over, he kissed her cheek.

Silence invaded the room. Ian glanced at Lilly. Her eyes were closed, her bottom lip caught between her teeth. He started to reach for her hand, but stopped himself. He could understand that she needed a few minutes of quiet.

The door opened and a nurse peeked in. "She's starting to wake up if you want to come into recovery. As soon as she's ready we'll move her to the third floor. We might wait until later this evening before we do that. We want to keep an eye on her."

Lilly's eyes were open now. She smiled and thanked the nurse as she reached to grab her purse. Ian stood up, flexing his shoulders to relieve the kinks in his muscles.

"You don't have to stay." Lilly stopped at the door. It hurt, a little, but he brushed it off. One thing he understood about Lilly was her need for independence.

"I know I don't have to stay. I want to stay. For Shelby, and for you."

"Thank you for getting her here and for taking care of her, Ian."

The false bravado in her tone was one he knew well. Or maybe it wasn't false. Lilly was one of the strongest women he knew. She had taken on the burden of a family long before she should have had those responsibilities.

He reached out, taking her shoulders in his hands before he leaned his forehead against hers. For a very long moment they stood like that, the same way they had as kids when Lilly had needed comfort, but hadn't been willing to be touched, or to let him get too close emotionally.

This time she pulled away. There was a filmy mist in her eyes as she turned from him.

"I need to be with Shelby."

Ian reached for the door. "Lilly, if you don't want me here, I'll leave."

She shook her head as they walked out into the hall. "I want you here."

Somehow it didn't feel like a victory.

CHAPTER 10

Lilly had been sitting next to her niece's bed for almost two hours. The little girl had slept most of that time. Ian sat across the room, making the plastic chair he was sitting in look almost comfortable. He had his legs stretched out in front of him, his arms behind his head, and he had even dozed once or twice.

She envied the fact that he seemed able to relax in almost any situation.

"I need a cup of coffee." Lilly stood up, stretched, and then looked down at the sleeping form of her niece.

"I'll get you one." Ian was on his feet, tall, lanky, and taking up too much of her space.

"No, I need to walk. I'm tired of sitting."

"Are you hungry? I could have them send up something."

"No, I'm not hungry." She edged past him. Instead of sitting, he followed her out of the room.

Lilly looked both ways, feeling uncomfortable with the idea of leaving Shelby alone for even a minute. An armed security officer looked up when they walked out of the room.

"She's safe, Lilly," Ian assured her.

"I know she is."

He reached for her hand. "The vending machines are down the hall, but I bet Anne has coffee in the nurses' station. She keeps hers fresh."

"That sounds good."

They walked down the fluorescent-lit hall, past darkened rooms. Brightly painted murals covered the walls, pictures of children playing, dogs running, and families on picnics. It could have been any pediatric ward in any hospital. And this time Shelby was the patient.

"Dr. Ian, is that you?" a small voice called from one room.

Ian stopped, and turned back to the room. "It's me, Tony. What are you doing up so late?"

Lilly followed him. A young boy inhabited the lone bed. The child smiled, exposing a missing tooth like any other child his age would have.

The shunt in his head was the only sign of illness. Lilly felt a familiar stirring of compassion. She had seen other children in his condition. And some worse.

"I couldn't sleep." Tony flipped off the cartoon channel he'd been watching. "I slept all day."

Ian sat down on the bed next to the little boy. He touched the child's cheek, and then patted his hand.

"Lonely, huh?"

The little boy nodded and then tears filled his eyes. "I don't want to be here alone."

Lilly felt tears burning her own eyes. She could sympathize with that feeling. She remembered how it felt to be a child and to feel alone.

"How about if I send Julie down here to sit with you for awhile? And later I'll come and sit with you." Ian offered the kind words with a smile.

Tony nodded, and wiped away the tears. Ian pulled a tissue from the box on the table and wiped away the remaining dampness. Watching the tender scene, Lilly's heart felt like it was being squeezed.

"Julie will be right down. And I'll have her bring you

some Jell-O." Ian winked at the child and patted his thin little arm.

Lilly followed Ian from the room. Somehow she felt as if she didn't know this man. When he was dressed in jeans and a T-shirt, cleaning out stalls, she knew him. But here, in this place, she found that she didn't really know him at all.

"He's a cute boy." She found words, something to make conversation that didn't include her confusion about Ian.

"Yes, he is."

"Why is he alone?" Lilly followed him into the cubicle that was the nurses' station. He poured a cup of coffee and handed it to her.

"He's in the custody of the state. He lives in a group home because there isn't a foster family willing to take him. He's either too much work, or they're afraid they'll get attached."

Lilly's already struggling heart shattered into a million pieces at the thought of that beautiful little boy going through so much and being so alone. Her life was jolted into perspective when compared to his.

"He's a great kid." Ian poured himself a cup of coffee. "I've considered trying to get custody of him."

"He would be a lucky boy if you did."

"I would be the lucky one." Ian stirred sugar into his coffee. "He's one of the happiest kids I've ever met."

Nurse Anne returned, smiling at them as she walked to her desk. Ian sat down across from her.

"What do you want?" Anne looked up from paperwork. Lilly chuckled. The older nurse obviously knew that smile on Ian's face.

"Tony's awake."

"And?"

"Do you think Julie could sit with him for a little while?"

Anne, kind-faced and with a halo of soft gray curls, nodded. "I'll send her down there. She's good with him."

"I know. She understands him." Ian stood up, and reached for his coffee. A scream echoed down the hall. Shelby's scream.

Lilly ran. She didn't care that Ian was behind her. She didn't care that she was in a hospital. Nothing mattered. Nothing but Shelby.

The security officer was already in the room when Lilly raced through the door. Lilly ignored him as she hurried to her niece's side.

"What is it, honey?" Lilly brushed tear-dampened curls from the child's flushed cheeks.

"My daddy. My daddy said he was going to take me away from you."

"No, Shelby, he isn't. Your daddy isn't here. And nobody's going to take you."

Shelby continued to cry. "He was here, he was standing here. And he was so mad."

Lilly shook her head, fighting against the unreasonable fear that was growing in the pit of her stomach.

Ian touched her shoulder. Lilly glanced at him, but then turned her attention back to the child in the bed.

"Nobody came in here, Lilly." He whispered the assurance. "The guard was here the whole time. He said nobody came in or out."

"But she's so afraid."

"It's the medication. She might have dreamed it, and maybe the dream seemed real."

Lilly nodded, knowing that he was right. Shelby looked up, her tears drying, but her lips still quivered.

"I'm scared, Aunt Lilly."

"It's okay, Shelby. We're here, and you're safe."

Lilly took a deep breath. When she did an acrid odor invaded her senses. It was a bitter, dirty smell. The smell of her ex-brother-in-law. She told herself it was her imagination. The guard hadn't seen anyone.

"You didn't go anywhere?" She didn't want to sound accusing; worse than that, she didn't want to see the guilty look in the young man's eyes.

"Just for a cup of coffee in the vending machine. It's only twenty feet from the door. He didn't have time . . ."

Lilly pressed her fingers against her eyes and shook her head. "You can't do that. Not even for a second."

"I'm sorry." He looked it, and he sounded it. Lilly sighed at the whipped look on his young face.

"I understand. I know you need breaks. I should have thought of that."

"I won't leave her again."

Shelby's eyes were already closing again. From time to time she sobbed, but the tears were gone. With the ease of childhood, she had forgotten the dream, and her fears.

Lilly needed more time.

But Carl. He was in the hospital. She could see the same thought registering on Ian's face. He reached for the phone and dialed a number. Lilly leaned her forehead against the window and listened to him tell the head of security about Carl's presence in the building.

"You need to get some sleep." Ian walked up behind her after he ended the call. His hands were on her shoulders. Lilly started to say something, but the words froze in her throat when he kissed the back of her head. She closed her eyes and waited for the world to right itself.

"Ian . . ."

"Don't argue, Lilly. You need to keep your strength up.

You can't take care of her if you let yourself get sick."

"I know." She moved away from him, back to her chair on the opposite side of the bed. "How can I sleep knowing that Carl could still be in here somewhere?"

"Get some sleep. I'm here. The guard is here."

The guard's presence no longer made her feel secure. The pungent smell of body odor still lingered.

But sleep was so tempting. Her body begged her to give in to its demands. Just a few minutes. She would close her eyes and rest for just a few minutes.

As she dozed off she felt a kiss, light as a feather, on her cheek. A blanket dropped over her shoulders and then she heard the soft thud of the door closing.

The sound of country music drew Lilly back to her surroundings. She stretched, pulled the blanket up around her face and slowly opened her eyes. It took a moment to adjust to the dimly lit hospital room.

In the soft gray of early morning she studied the sleeping face of her niece, and then her eyes focused on the TV, and the country music videos that played like a quiet backdrop in the silent room.

A rustling sound drew her gaze to the man sitting in the corner of the room. Ian sat with his bare feet propped up on the windowsill. At first she thought he might be sleeping. And then she realized that he was watching her.

"Hey, sleeping beauty."

"Please don't tell me you're the handsome prince."

He chuckled. "I've been called a lot of things, but never handsome and never a prince."

Lilly smiled. She started to respond, but Shelby stirred in the bed, mumbling about her mommy. Lilly felt a stab in the region of her heart. She brushed a hand across her forehead and carefully avoided looking at Ian.

She couldn't be strong if she saw pity in his eyes. And at the moment any strength she thought she possessed felt sadly inadequate for the situation.

"Lilly, you can make it through this. You're one of the strongest women that I know. Look at what you've done with your life."

She looked up at the ceiling and blinked away the tears that tried to form in her eyes. When she looked at Ian she managed to feel almost composed. She even found a smile, hoping it would be enough to convince them both that she was in control.

Her attention turned to the window, and she looked out at the peaceful scene of the sleepy town she'd grown up in just starting to come to life for the day.

"We're here to help you, Lilly."

She listened to Ian's words, and felt a warm glow that matched the light of the sun just peeking over the eastern horizon. This was why she had come back to Gardner, because she wanted people in Shelby's life who would care about her.

She wanted it for Shelby. And even for herself. Especially at times like this, when it felt so good to have someone to lean on, and to share her concerns with. At the same time, it scared her, knowing how much she had come to rely on them.

"I've let you help me," she protested weakly.

"Of course you have, and you've fought it every step of the way."

She smiled at him, shrugging her shoulders in acknowledgement of his words. "Yes, I guess I have."

Two days later Ian walked behind Lilly as she pushed

Shelby in a wheelchair toward the front entrance of the hospital. A nurse's aide walked to the side of them, keeping up a steady stream of chatter about the weather and how nice it would be for Shelby to play outside again.

The memory of a phone call he had overheard the previous night replayed in his mind, and the voice of the nurse's aide faded.

"I won't let you take her, Carl. If I have to, I'll run. You won't find us." Lilly's voice had sounded strong, but Ian had heard the thread of panic in her tone.

She would run. She would leave them, and leave Oklahoma. And he wouldn't be able to stop her. He knew it, but he didn't want to accept the possibility.

Somehow he would keep them safe.

A car pulled past them. Ian moved closer to the women, hoping that Lilly wouldn't notice that he was sticking close to her side.

"Where's your truck?"

Ian looked away from the car circling the parking lot. "What? I'm sorry, I wasn't paying attention."

"Because you're watching every car in the parking lot." Lilly sighed. "Ian, I can't live like this."

Her words were spoken softly, low enough to keep Shelby from catching what they were discussing. Ian wanted to avoid the topic, and what she meant by those words. "We shouldn't discuss this right now."

"Ian, I mean it."

"We can talk later." He pulled his keys out of his pocket. "My truck is over there."

He pointed to his truck, and Lilly turned to the right, following the sidewalk that skirted the parking lot. The nurse's aide was still chattering to Shelby, distracting her with meaningless conversation.

Ian wished he could be distracted. He didn't want to think about the days ahead or what could happen. He wanted Shelby safe. He wanted Lilly to stay in Oklahoma.

He prayed that he wouldn't have to let them go.

CHAPTER 11

Shelby sat in the yard with the puppy Ian had brought home the previous day. He insisted the blue heeler pup was his, but Lilly saw it as another small chink in her armor. How could she say no to Shelby, to a child who had been through so much?

"She's doing so well. Hard to believe it's only been a week." Kathy set down the casserole she had brought down for them.

A week. Lilly didn't find it hard to believe. The days had been long. The nights since they had come home had been longer, mostly sleepless. Noises were magnified in the quiet country nights. Lilly spent the wee hours of the morning pacing through her house, peeking out the windows and looking off into the dark for any sign of Carl.

As daylight would spread its pink glow across the eastern horizon she would crash next to Shelby and sleep until her niece stirred. And now she slept until the puppy whined.

Kathy rubbed Lilly's shoulder. "Don't worry so much, Lilly. You can't change things by worrying."

"I know." She tapped on the window, a warning to Shelby to not get too rough. The child smiled and waved. The puppy saw its chance and escaped.

"She's so beautiful. I really see Missy in her." Kathy watched out the window, a smile spreading across her face. "You girls didn't have a fair shake in this world. But you survived it. She'll survive it too."

"But what about Missy?" Lilly wanted to take the words

145

back. She didn't want to share her guilt with anyone. It was hers, she could handle it.

"Oh, honey." Kathy wrapped a motherly arm around her. "You did your best for that girl. You worked so hard, trying to make things better. She made her own choices."

"I shouldn't have taken her so far from home. If we'd stayed here . . ."

"Don't do that to yourself. You had no way of knowing. Hindsight is a twenty-twenty thing, and it's bunk. You can't know for sure that things would have been better if you had stayed. Do you think people here don't get into trouble?"

"I know they do, but what if Missy hadn't?"

"Life is full of what ifs." Kathy patted Lilly's arm. "You can't do this to yourself. You have to find faith. Let God do the worrying."

"I just want Shelby to be happy. I want her to have a chance."

"That's why you brought her back here? Why, honey, you know the people here will love her. And you'll give her every opportunity."

"Please pray for me, Kathy. I never know if I'm doing the right thing. I prayed that I'd make the right decision and I really felt as though this was the path God wanted me to take. And now, almost daily, I wonder if I should have stayed in Kansas City, or gone somewhere else."

"I'll pray for you. And you trust God. He's seen you through a lot and He'll get you through this."

A knock on the front door ended their conversation. Lilly looked out the front window and saw Ian's truck. She crossed the room to let him in. He'd gone back to work when she moved back into her house. Funny, she had sort of missed him.

"Hey, how are my favorite ladies." Ian winked as he

leaned to kiss Kathy's cheek. When he turned to Lilly he stopped. She drew in a deep breath, waiting, and was almost disappointed when he didn't kiss her.

Now, how silly was that?

"Oh, honey, we're all just fine," Kathy answered for them. "I'm making you cinnamon rolls. You're on your own for dinner, though."

"That's fine. I can take care of myself."

Lilly's gaze traveled to the casserole dish on her table. She could invite him to join them. Shelby would like that.

"You could join us. I think Kathy brought us the dinner she meant for you."

Kathy laughed at that. "Yes, but I left him the cinnamon rolls."

"That sounds good. And I'll even bring the cinnamon rolls down here for dessert. If you'll make the coffee."

"It's a date." She choked when the words came out. "I mean, that sounds good."

"But it definitely won't be a date," Ian teased.

Lilly ignored his grin. She followed Kathy as the older woman headed for the front door.

"Kathy, thank you so much for bringing us dinner."

"You're welcome, sweetie. And thank my boss. He came up with the idea."

Lilly heard Ian mutter a quiet "uh-oh" as Kathy walked out the door. When she turned, he was retreating to the back door and the safety of the yard where Shelby was playing with the puppy.

"So, what are you cooking up in here?"

Lilly started at Ian's voice behind her. She had been so absorbed in reading over the recipe, she hadn't noticed when he walked into the kitchen. She glanced over her shoulder and smiled at him. He was leaning against the counter, his arms crossed over his chest.

He had no right, making her feel so content—like life was meant to be like this, with the two of them together in her kitchen. She offered him a smile and went back to the cookbook. "It's a surprise."

"Code for *I'm not sure yet.*" He laughed at his own joke, such an annoying habit. She laughed, too.

"Exactly."

She moved a few glasses into the sink, and ran dishwater. Ian moved next to her, leaning his elbows on the counter. The earthy scent of his cologne swirled around her. She peeked at him out of the corner of her eye. He had gone home to take a shower and his hair curled in damp rings at the nape of his neck. The slacks he had worn had been traded for jeans and a T-shirt.

Warning bells went off in her mind. *Sensory overload, sensory overload, man has entered the comfort zone. Alert. Step away and nobody will get hurt.*

She tried to ignore him as she turned to a recipe for something with whipped cream and chocolate. A quick glance at the ingredients told her it had to be good.

"Sounds great to me." Ian, reading over her shoulder, offered his opinion. "But I really could have brought the cinnamon rolls back with me."

"We'll eat those tomorrow. If you don't eat them all for breakfast. I just feel like cooking something." Contrary. She knew how to be contrary. He only laughed. He knew her too well.

"I'll leave now. If I keep giving my opinions, you'll make something with butterscotch just to spite me."

"Probably. So go play with Shelby and that dog of yours."

"Shelby's dog," he admitted as he walked away. "How could you possibly tell her no?"

"I could, but I wouldn't win."

He shrugged, slid his bare feet into the flip-flops he had worn and walked out the back door. Lilly watched him go and then she let out a long sigh. He was getting to her. She didn't know if he knew it or not, but day by day her defenses were crumbling.

The "no cowboys" rule was getting fuzzy around the edges.

"This is wonderful." Ian took the last bite of the chocolate dessert. "I had no idea you could cook like this."

"You don't really know me, now, do you?"

"Oh, I think I do." He smiled at Shelby. The little girl's head was bobbing over the macaroni and cheese that Lilly had made for her. "I think someone has had enough. I'll carry her to the bedroom."

"I'll make coffee."

He picked Shelby up and she wrapped chubby arms around his neck. It felt more like she was wrapping herself around his heart. It would be hard, letting them go if Lilly decided to leave. And what if Lilly left without saying good-bye?

He pushed the bedroom door open with his shoulder and crossed the room, easing Shelby down on the bed and then pulling a blanket over her. She smiled up at him, a smile that was pure innocence. She could have asked him for anything, and he would have had a hard time telling her no.

"I love you, Ian," she whispered in the soft lisp of early childhood.

"I love you, too." He kissed her forehead. "Go to sleep. We're right outside if you need anything."

"Will you leave the light on?" Her bottom lip quivered.

"Of course I will." He sat down on the edge of the bed. "Do you want me to sing to you?"

She nodded. He sang softly, watching as her eyes grew heavy, fluttered and then closed in sleep. When he stood up and turned toward the door, Lilly was there. Her smile threw him off guard.

"You sing better than I do," she whispered as he walked out of the room. "I made coffee."

She smiled at him, another genuine smile. It was the kind of smile that made him hope, especially as they walked down the hall together, his arm around her waist and his heart wrapped around her little finger.

"Coffee." Lilly walked on to the porch with the tray. She set it down on the table between their chairs. Ian she ignored. For the moment she didn't want to look at him.

"This is great." His words forced her attention to his face, to his smile. Her heart twitched and did a triple back flip in her chest, landing with a thud against her ribs. Funny, but the chaos she used to feel in Ian's presence had turned to tranquility.

How had that happened? Or maybe it had nothing to do with Ian. Maybe the serenity was found in the hazy pink twilight and the sweet call of the birds. Maybe it had nothing to do with a liquid-gold gaze fringed with dark lashes, or the comfort she felt in Ian's presence.

That had to be it: quiet country nights, not Ian. Just recognizing that fact made her feel better.

"I do love nights like this. I didn't realize how much I had missed the quiet of the country." Lilly sat down in her chair and put her feet up on the porch railing.

"It is a good place to be. I could have left, but I couldn't imagine being anywhere but here."

"I hadn't planned to come back here," she admitted.

"I know, but you are here now and it'll work out. I wanted to let you know that we're going to have an opening in pediatrics."

"I need a job, but I can't do it yet. Not until I know what is going to happen."

He didn't respond, didn't even argue. She had expected him to tell her to stay, to let him help. Instead he nodded and then took a sip of his coffee.

And she felt oddly let down.

The soft sound of early evening closed in on them as dusk settled over the valley. Lilly closed her eyes, enjoying the warm air and the light breeze that caressed her skin.

She heard Ian move from his seat and she opened her eyes. He reached out, and she let him take her hand. His fingers wrapped around hers and he pulled her up to stand in front of him.

Lilly's breath caught in her lungs as she reached to touch his cheek. Warm air, the scent of roses, and Ian's hazel eyes promising her something that she felt she couldn't have.

His face descended, his lips lowered to touch hers. A butterfly kiss, as gentle and whispery as the late autumn breeze that blew from the south. The perfect moment, the perfect kiss, and no regrets. Lilly closed her eyes and leaned her forehead against Ian's shoulder. Her heart melted into her feet and her will to fight the emotions of that moment fled under his gentle touch.

Ian moved, brushing his cheek against the top of her head. "Whatever happens, Lilly, it'll be okay. I just want you to know that."

The shrill ring of the telephone shattered the moment and the stillness of the night. Lilly jumped, the sudden movement making her insides tremble and her hands shake. She reached for the phone as Ian moved back to his chair.

"Hi, Lilly, it's me, Carl." The hiss of her ex-brother-in-law's voice chilled her from the inside out, and the warmth she had felt only seconds earlier dissolved. "That's a very sweet boyfriend. Maybe you should have been watching Shelby."

A click and the line went dead.

Panic surged through Lilly as the sickening implication threaded through her numbed mind. She tossed the phone down on the table and ran into the house. Ian ran after her; she heard his feet pounding across the floor as he followed.

"Lilly, what is it?"

He whispered, but the words seemed so loud in the stillness of the empty house. Lilly shook her head, she couldn't talk to him, couldn't explain her fear, irrational as it might be. She raced down the hall to the bedroom where Shelby slept.

At the door to the room she stopped. Leaning against the door frame, she sobbed quietly into her hands. Ian's arms were around her and he pulled her back into the hall.

"She's here. Oh, Ian, I thought . . . he wanted me to think he had taken Shelby." She sobbed against the soft cotton of his T-shirt.

Ian wrapped an arm around her and led her back to the living room. She sat down, still trying to make sense of Carl's threats, the sick game he was playing with her. Ian left her alone for a minute. She watched as he checked to make sure all of the doors were locked.

Lilly needed to be doing something. She should pack their suitcases, do the dishes, find her purse— something proactive. She shouldn't be sitting in a chair waiting for Ian to take control and keep them safe.

"He's playing a game, Lilly. We aren't going to let him win. He wants you scared. He wants you on the run."

Lilly felt a chilling realization. "He wants me to feel what he feels. He wants me afraid. He wants me on the run."

"And we're not going to let him do that." He sat down next to her and took her hand in his. "Don't run, Lilly."

"I don't know, Ian. As long as Carl is out there, we'll never feel safe. I'll always worry that he might take her from me."

"You can't let him control you this way. Don't run. Stay and let's find a way to catch him."

"I'm not going . . ." She stood up, looking around her living room that only an hour earlier had seemed like a restful haven to her. "Okay, I've considered leaving. I'm so tired of wondering where he is "

"I don't want you to leave." Ian followed her to the front door. She looked out the window, knowing he was there with her. "Lilly, I've missed you."

"Ian, I can't go there with you."

"I'm not asking. I know how you feel. I want your friendship, Lilly. I won't push you into something you don't want." He grinned. "At least you know I'm not just a cowboy."

His humor lightened her mood. She even managed to smile. "I'm a little sorry that I lost that excuse."

"Lilly, not all cowboys hurt the people they love. Most of them take care of their families."

Lilly turned away from the window, but avoided looking into his eyes, knowing he wanted understanding from her. "Don't, Ian. Please don't start that. Right now it isn't about cowboys, or living in Oklahoma. My main concern is Shelby."

Ian joined her in the kitchen. As she started running

water in the sink, she heard the clatter of dishes and knew that he was clearing the table.

"And what about you, Lilly?" He set the stack of dishes on the counter. "If you take care of Missy and Shelby, who takes care of you?"

"The same person who has always taken care of me—I take care of myself."

Ian rinsed his hands in the water. "I need to go outside. If Carl is out there, I'm going to try and find him. And you keep the doors locked and the alarm on."

She pretended not to watch him leave, but she did. His reflection in the window painted a picture for her of a man who only wanted her understanding. He wanted to be there for her. As he walked out the front door, she wiped a single tear from her cheek with a soap-covered hand.

Ian grabbed a flashlight from his truck and then he started a careful trek around the house, widening his path as he walked. If Carl was hiding on this farm, Ian would find him.

Dark had completely engulfed the valley and Lilly's old farmhouse when he hiked back down the hill. The front porch light glowed a dim yellow, throwing a circle of light onto the yard.

From inside the house Ian heard the sharp bark of the pup trying to be the guard dog he would never be. Ian walked up the front steps and the door opened. Lilly blocked the entrance.

"Where have you been?"

"I told you I was going to look for Carl."

She didn't invite him in, and he wasn't surprised. What surprised him was the puffiness around her eyes. If he didn't know better, he would guess that she'd been crying. He knew better than to ask.

"You were gone a long time." She stepped out the door and joined him on the porch. "I was almost worried."

"Almost?"

"Only a little."

The flash of blue coming down the road took him by surprise. "You called the police?"

"I told Dean he needed to come and see if you were dead out there."

"I'm flattered."

"Don't be. Now, since you've rescued yourself and Dean is here, I'm going inside."

He started to tell her that he didn't want her to stay in the house alone. He almost told her that he was worried. The look on her face stopped him in his tracks. It wouldn't do to tangle with her, not in her present mood.

He glanced toward Dean's car, and the door behind him shut with a firm thud. So, that was that. He walked down the steps and met his friend in the yard.

"She's mad?" Dean chuckled and shook his head. "You do, do have a way with women."

"Thank you, I think. I checked the whole property. I didn't see a sign of Carl anywhere." He walked with Dean to his truck. "So, did she tell you why she's so mad?"

"Scared, I think. She'd rather be mad than worried about you."

This time Ian laughed. "Yeah, I guess you're right about that. So, do you want to stop by the house for a cup of coffee?"

Dean shrugged. "Sure."

Before he backed out of the drive, Ian gave the yard one last look. His gaze landed on the front window. Lilly was watching. He waved, even though she couldn't see him.

As he drove away he prayed that she would be protected,

and that God would help them to find Carl before he could hurt Shelby.

The old church that Lilly had attended as a child still held services each Sunday. The white wood siding had been replaced with brick. The parking lot had been paved, and an addition had been built at the back of the building. Time had a way of changing things, sometimes for the better.

Lilly waited in front of Ian's truck. Shelby ran up to her, holding out her arms to be carried. Lilly picked her up and held her tight.

"She can walk," he admonished.

"I know, but I want to carry her." Silly Lilly, needing a shield to protect her from curious glances and questions that she didn't want to answer. Not that Shelby could protect her.

"I'll carry her," Ian offered.

Shelby reached for him even as Lilly tried to protest. Too late. She'd lost the battle before it began. Sick apprehension knotted in her stomach as they moved toward the sidewalk. People were gathered on the front lawn, laughing and smiling. The bell tolled, telling them that church would start in ten minutes. The crowd continued to talk.

"Hey, Lilly." The feminine voice accosted her before she could escape. Lilly turned, releasing a relieved sigh when she saw that it was Jamie.

"Jamie, I've been meaning to get out to see you again." She hugged her friend.

"Is that why you look like a cornered 'possum?"

Laughter eased the tension. Jamie had always been good at finding humor in what appeared to be the worst situations.

"A cornered 'possum? Now that's a new one." Ian entered the conversation. "But then, Jamie has always been good at being unique. So why *do* you look like a cornered 'possum, Lil?"

"I've just been gone a long time."

How could she explain about her fears for herself and for Shelby? More than anything she wanted her niece to have a normal childhood, one that didn't include humiliation over the mistakes her parents had made, or teasing because her clothes weren't new or the right size.

A trio of older women swarmed them, wearing beehive hairdos and welcoming smiles that enveloped Lilly as effectively as a hug.

"Land sakes, Lilly Tanner, you're all grown up and so beautiful." The older of the three, Mrs. Witt, patted her cheek.

"Looks just like her beautiful mother. I had her in Sunday school nearly forty years ago." The second woman smiled tenderly as she imparted this piece of news.

And Lilly realized then that the past was the past. Somewhere along the way she had stopped being "that poor Lilly Tanner," and she had become an adult, the daughter of "that beautiful Jackson girl."

But what about Shelby? How would they handle the truth about Missy?

It took a few minutes to escape the crowd of people who wanted to welcome her back into the fold. Lilly smiled, accepted their hugs, and wondered why now? Why hadn't they gathered around her when she was eighteen, alone with a fourteen-year-old sister and her mother wasted away from a broken heart and too much alcohol?

Maybe the fault was hers? Maybe she had pushed them away, wanting to take care of everything herself? That hurt more than the thought that they had rejected her. She glanced in Ian's direction and thought of all of the times she had pushed him away, fearing that he would let her down.

When she reached for his hand, he blinked a few times before closing his fingers around hers. She smiled at the surprised look on his face, and her heart did a happy dance in her chest.

The bell rang the final warning. Lilly took a deep breath and followed Ian into church with Shelby at her side.

"Do you want me to take Shelby to her Sunday school class?" he offered.

"No, I want to go with her. You can show us where."

Ian nodded and led them through the church to the classrooms at the back of the building. The first door to the left was the preschool/kindergarten classroom, just as it had been twenty-five years ago.

Lilly stepped through the door and back into the past, into warm memories of vacation Bible school, butterscotch oatmeal cookies and loving hugs. Security. Funny how that one word defined her childhood memories of this place and covered up other memories of children who had teased because her feet were bare, or adults who had whispered about her father as she passed by them in the hall.

Security overshadowed those other feelings, and even helped the scars to fade.

She wanted that security and healing for Shelby. Maybe more than she wanted her own life in Kansas City. Or maybe she wanted this place for herself, too.

"Lilly Tanner, imagine seeing you back here."

Lilly was just as amazed, and she didn't know who the woman was that had hold of Shelby's hand. Gray eyes, curling long blond hair. The woman held out a well-manicured hand.

"You don't remember me."

Lilly didn't, but she wished she did. She didn't know the

woman who appeared to be about ten years her senior, but she liked her, and had probably liked her in the past.

"Jenny Gartin. Well, it's Jenny Douglas now." The woman shook Lilly's outstretched hand. And suddenly Lilly remembered. She remembered being seven, and falling on the playground at school. A teenager, pretty, and dressed in finer clothes than Lilly had ever seen, picked her up and took her inside to the nurse. The teenager, Jenny Gartin, had even stayed with her, holding her hand while the nurse put salve on the scrapes.

"Jenny, I'm sorry, I should have remembered you."

"Oh, are you kidding me? Of course you shouldn't have. I went away to college when you were still in grade school."

"It doesn't seem like that long ago." Lilly reached for Shelby's hand. "And this is my niece Shelby. She'll be in your class today."

Jenny kneeled on the floor next to Shelby, a welcoming smile on her face that would have warmed any child. And Shelby was no exception. As Lilly walked out of the room, she could hear her niece talking about her surgery, the puppy, and riding ponies, and how Ian was the best uncle in the world.

CHAPTER 12

"That isn't really your mom. My mom said your mom is in jail."

Lilly heard the words, but she wanted to believe she hadn't. They were sitting in a restaurant having Sunday lunch with several families from church. It wasn't supposed to be this way. Shelby was supposed to be protected here.

"Lilly, relax." Ian's hand touched her arm. She jerked her head around to look at him, unable to focus on his face or his reassurances. "She's a child. She doesn't understand."

"Her parents should. They should know better."

"True, but you can't run every time someone says something you don't like."

"I have to leave." Lilly stood up. "I'm sorry, Ian. Shelby, we need to leave now."

Shelby looked up, blinking a few times in surprise. "But you said I could have ice cream."

"Lilly, let her have ice cream."

"I want to leave, Ian. You can stay."

Ian tossed a couple of bills on the table. "You rode with me."

She heard him, but she was already busy gathering up her things, and Shelby. People were staring. She knew that they were whispering. Common sense told her to stay, but her hurt feelings wouldn't allow it. She had spent her childhood being teased. She remembered hurtful words about her dad being a drunk. She didn't want that for Shelby.

They were almost to the truck when Debbie, the mother

of the little girl, caught up with them.

"Lilly, please, let me apologize. I'm so sorry that Claire said what she did. She's only five, she didn't mean any harm. She heard me tell Jim about Missy. We were talking. It wasn't meant to hurt anyone."

Lilly relaxed her grip on Shelby's hand and somehow she smiled. Her heartbeat returned to something close to its normal pace, and she felt her face cooling in the light breeze that had picked up, blowing a few storm clouds their way.

"I really am sorry." Debbie touched her arm. "I wouldn't hurt you or Shelby for anything."

"I know you wouldn't."

"Please forgive us."

Lilly nodded. "I forgive you."

"Can I have my ice cream?" Shelby's small voice interrupted.

Lilly smiled down at her. "Not this time, kiddo. We'll stop and get something to take home with us. I have a headache and I just really want to go home."

Lilly ignored the questioning looks that Ian tossed her way. She could do without his nonverbal lectures. She could chastise herself without his help.

Ian kept his mouth shut, but it wasn't easy. He understood why Lilly reacted the way she had. He had heard the taunting she received in school. It hadn't been easy for her.

"Go ahead and say it." She continued to stare out the side window of the truck as she rubbed her temples with her fingers.

"I wasn't going to say anything." He glanced in the rearview mirror and saw that Shelby had fallen asleep. She had her stuffed dog under her chin and her thumb stuck in her mouth.

"I acted like an idiot." Lilly was facing him now, her face

161

slightly pale and damp from perspiration.

"Lilly, you acted like a mother who wanted to protect her child. But you have to realize that no matter what a person's situation, there's always the chance they could be teased. If you have money, kids will tease you about that. If you have two parents, they'll find something about your parents. If you live in the wrong house or the right house, it just doesn't matter. What matters is what you feel about yourself."

"Right now I feel like my head is splitting, and to top it off I acted like an idiot."

"You reacted to the memories of your childhood. But remember: because of you, Shelby will have a good childhood. Teach her to believe in herself so that she won't believe what other people think or say."

"How'd you get to be so wise?" She leaned against the window. "Ian, I'm going to be sick."

And before he could pull over, she was.

The shrill ringing of the telephone jarred Lilly from the soundest sleep she'd had in weeks. She jumped from the bed, and then realized that it wasn't her house or her phone. She sat back down on the edge of the bed and waited for her body to wake up and to stop trembling after its rude awakening.

She was in the spare bedroom at Ian's house. He had brought her there after she totally ruined the carpet in his truck. He had given her medicine, bathed her head with a cool cloth, and then led her upstairs to the room she had slept in when she first arrived in Gardner.

He hadn't complained about the truck, or told her that she was too much trouble. Ian wasn't her dad. Ian always managed to be there for her when she needed him. Ian had never let her down.

She leaned back on the pillow, wishing her thoughts made more sense. She had a job to do. She was here to take care of Shelby, not to get involved with a cowboy—especially a bull-riding cowboy. She couldn't risk that.

She couldn't risk losing him. The unbidden thought shook her more than being shaken from a sound sleep.

She lifted her arm and squinted at the numbers on her watch. Only six in the morning. But if she remembered right, she'd been sleeping since seven the previous night.

What a horrible way to start a Monday.

She sat up again and put her feet on the soft wool rug at the side of the bed. The thought of curling back up in the bed tempted her, but the aroma of fresh-brewed coffee drifted into her room, offering a stronger temptation.

Before going downstairs, she tiptoed into Shelby's room to check on her. The little girl lay curled up in the center of the bed, the down comforter wrapped around her shoulders and her thumb stuck in her mouth. Lilly leaned, started to kiss the rosy pink of the child's cheek, but then thought better of it. No reason to wake her so early.

Ian looked up when she walked into the kitchen. He held the phone between his cheek and shoulder and wrote down numbers with his free hand. Lilly poured herself a cup of coffee and sat down next to him.

"Dad, I'll pick you up." Ian nodded, as if the person on the other end of the phone could see. "No, don't rent a car. Why would you rent a car when you know that I'm only thirty minutes from Tulsa?"

Lilly left the room and walked outside to watch the sunrise. She didn't want to be in the middle of a father-son discussion. She shivered in the crisp October morning. The damp air seeped into her bones more than it should have.

The door behind her opened. She smiled at Ian and then

turned her attention back to the pale pink, lavender and touch of gray that streaked across the eastern horizon just as the sun came up.

"My parents are coming to visit me." He offered to refill her cup with the carafe of coffee he had carried out of the house, and then he set it on the table.

"You sound thrilled." Lilly sat down in one of the Adirondack chairs, and Ian took the other.

"I love them, but usually when they come to see me it's for a reason. They don't visit just to be visiting."

"I see." But she didn't. She hadn't had parents, not real ones, since early childhood. Sometimes she felt as if she had been the adult in her family her entire life.

It got tiring, always being the grown-up, the one who could handle any situation, who would always be responsible. But if she wasn't that person, who would be?

"Lilly, are you still with me?" Ian's hand covered hers, his was warm and hers felt like ice. She didn't follow that first instinct to move away, but instead accepted the warmth that seeped into her body from his touch.

"I'm here, just thinking about you, your parents . . ." She didn't finish. She didn't want his sympathy.

"I'm sorry, sometimes I forget." His fingers tightened around hers in a gentle squeeze.

"It isn't your fault." She offered him a weak smile. "Thank you for last night, for taking care of me."

"You're welcome. Do you feel like eating something?"

"No, I don't think so." She lifted her cup of coffee and drained the contents. "I need to go home. I don't think it would be good if I was here when your parents got here. I don't think your mother has ever liked me."

"She doesn't dislike you."

"I love that you think that, but I really do want to go

home. I have so much to do around that place to get it ready for winter."

"I could help."

"I know, and you can. But you need to see your parents." She looked at her empty coffee cup. "Ian, you need to make amends with them."

For a moment he remained silent. She chanced a glance in his direction. His attention focused on the rising of the sun, the faint glow of pink on the horizon.

"I know it isn't any of my business."

He smiled. "No, it isn't, but we do tend to make each other's lives our business. You're right, though. I lecture you about letting go of the past, but I'm hanging on to the memories of my parents keeping me in classes, moving me forward ahead of my friends, and then starting me in college long before I was ready emotionally."

"It had to be rough for you. I wish I had known."

He shrugged. "I'm glad you didn't. I needed you to be the person you were in my life."

Lilly rested her hand on his arm, feeling something stronger than what she had always considered friendship.

Lilly didn't scream when she walked into her house, but that was her first reaction. Shelby's presence next to her forced her to be calm.

"Aunt Lilly, what happened to our house?"

Lilly shook her head as her gaze slid over the destruction of her home. The walls were painted red, and her furniture had been slashed to shreds. The pictures had been pulled off the walls and smashed to pieces.

"I don't know, sweetie. Let's just walk back outside to the car." She held tight to her niece's hand and retreated to the safety of her van.

165

Lilly helped Shelby into the seat, and climbed in behind her. She pulled the door shut and hit the lock button. Shelby climbed back to her seat, sobbing softly into the fur of her stuffed animal.

The cell phone rang. Lilly reached for it, her hands shaking as she flipped it open and held it to her ear.

"Welcome home, Lilly. Do you like how I decorated your house?"

"Where are you?" Lilly scanned the horizon looking for any sign of Carl.

"If I told you where I was hiding, it would ruin the game. I like it better this way."

As strong as she wanted to be, Lilly couldn't stop shaking. Her body trembled from the inside out and her hands shook so hard she could barely hold the phone.

"Leave us alone, Carl. Just leave. Shelby is fine with me. And if you keep this up, they'll catch you."

Where was he, and why couldn't they find him? How could he hide like this?

"Like I care. You took my wife, and you took my business. I'm not going to leave, Lilly, not yet."

Lilly reached for the key that she'd left in the ignition. She cranked the engine to life, shifted into reverse and spun around in the driveway until her car was pointing up the hill. She threw the van into drive and hit the accelerator.

"Aunt Lilly, where are we going?"

"To Ian's house." She dialed 911 as she drove. And she prayed. She might not know where Carl was hiding, but God did. She prayed that he would be found before he could do anything to hurt them.

Ian didn't mind silence, but when the silence was cool, filled with frowns, cautious glances, and his parents . . .

then the silence wasn't a wonderful thing. He glanced across the cab of the truck and smiled at his mother. She actually smiled back.

When he had helped her into his truck back at the airport she had sighed, a very heartfelt sigh, and asked him why he didn't spend some of his money and buy a nice car. He had explained that a truck suited his needs, and it was an extended cab, so it had room for friends.

Dad was almost as unhappy as Mom. He had at least tried to make some small talk. The typical, "Hi, son, how have you been? How is work?" sort of thing that had been the mainstay of every conversation they'd had in the last ten years.

"So, son, are you still raising horses?" Dad asked, and if Ian remembered correctly, the question had already been asked.

"Yes, still raising them."

They were only a tenth of a mile from his house now. The sight of Lilly's van pulling into his drive surprised him. But not as much as the sound of a siren coming up behind him. He pulled into the drive and waited for Dean's patrol car to come to a stop before he stepped out.

"What's going on?" he asked as he rounded the back of Lilly's van. She was pale, her hands shaking as she clasped them together.

"Carl," Dean answered as he opened the van door and reached for Shelby. The child wrapped her arms around the officer's neck.

"Lilly, take Shelby inside." The moment the words were out of his mouth, Ian knew his mistake. He had tried—really tried—not to look like he was taking over. For weeks he had teetered on the edge of success.

The flash of fire from Lilly's eyes told him that he'd overstepped the boundaries.

"It's my problem, Ian, my house that has been ransacked, and my life. I'll not go inside like a good girl."

Dean turned coward. "I'll take Shelby in to Kathy."

"Thanks, Dean." Ian motioned his parents forward. His mother had recognized Lilly. She didn't look disapproving, just surprised.

"Lilly, I didn't know you were back." Ian's mom held out her hand, and Lilly accepted the gesture. "It seems as if there is a problem. Dave and I will wait inside."

"Thanks, Mom." He watched them walk away before turning back to Lilly. "I apologize. I've tried so hard to give you space, Lilly. I didn't mean to take over."

She kicked at a stone on the drive, sending it bouncing across the pavement. "I know. But, Ian, I didn't come back here for this."

"For this?"

"For a relationship."

"I see." He couldn't stop the smile across his face. "Is that what this is?"

"I don't know. It isn't what I planned. I had planned on being strong. I wanted to come back here and start a new life for myself. That new life wasn't supposed to be about us, or about you taking care of me, it's supposed to be about Shelby and giving her a chance."

"I think I knew that."

"But you're taking over, and I can't let that happen. You confuse me, and I forget my priorities."

"Millions—no, billions—of people have relationships that include children and they don't forget their priorities."

"I can't help what other people do. I know what I have to do. I have to keep it together for a little girl who has lost everything. I can't put her through what I went through, always wondering if . . ."

He finally understood, maybe better than she did. He was looking at the little girl who had lost everything. She had lost her parents, her childhood, and now she was losing the security she had fought so hard to hang on to.

"Shelby hasn't lost everything, Lil. She has you. She has us."

"She lost her parents."

Her tears fell, coursing down her cheeks like a storm that had been kept at bay for too long. Ian took a step forward and she willingly walked into his arms. He held her tight until the tears ended and only dry sobs remained.

"I'm sorry that life has been so hard for you, Lilly. I should have done more."

"Stop, Ian. I don't want you to do more. I don't want to feel as though I can only survive if you're there to hold life together for me." She looked up, tears still shimmering in her eyes. "What if you were suddenly gone and I couldn't survive?"

"You're not your mother." And from the look on her face, he knew he had hit the target. He regretted that he'd said it. But maybe she needed to face that realization.

The front door opened and she pulled out of his arms. She brushed away the few remaining tears and managed to smile at Dean.

"They can't find him." Dean was wise enough to direct his comment to Lilly. "They've searched your house, the farm, the surrounding area."

"Thank you, Dean." She sighed, and looked at Ian. "So, what do I do?"

Ian pointed to himself, wondering if she really wanted him to answer. She frowned a warning.

"Stay here for a day or two. Give us time to search."

"Your parents are here."

"It's a big house."

169

Dean stepped away from the two of them. "I have a few places to check. Lilly . . . stay here."

And that settled it. From Dean it was an order, and even Lilly wouldn't argue.

Lilly followed Ian up the front walk, casting one last look in the direction of her house. Carl was out there some-where. As long as he was on the loose, Shelby wasn't safe. Lilly didn't know what she would do, but she knew that she needed to do something.

They walked through the empty great room of Ian's house, and found his parents in the kitchen with Shelby. Lilly stopped, awed by the sight of Ian's mother scooping out ice cream.

She shouldn't have been so surprised. Ian's mother had grown up on this farm. She must have gone barefoot, worked in the barn, and even waded in the creek. Somehow she managed to look as if she had never belonged here, but there must have been a time, a long time ago, when she had belonged here.

Lilly realized that maybe the two of them had more in common than she had ever realized.

"Is everything okay?" Ian's father pointed at an empty chair and Ian sat down.

"Fine. Lilly and Shelby are going to join us for a day or two."

"That will be nice." Elizabeth Hunt almost sounded as if she meant it.

"I need to go down to the house to see if there is any-thing salvageable. And I need to find the puppy."

"I'll take you down."

She had expected Ian's offer, but she didn't want to pull him away from his family. But the idea of going alone didn't appeal to her either.

"You stay here with your parents. I'm sure Johnny would go with me."

"Lilly, I'm going. Shelby can stay here with Mom and Kathy."

"Thank you, Ian." She smiled at his mother. "We won't be gone long."

She kissed Shelby on the cheek and told her to mind, and then she walked away, knowing that Ian followed.

Most of Lilly's clothes were ripped and tossed in the yard. Dirt had been poured into the sink and water run to clog the drain. Windows were broken and pictures were smashed. It looked like an Oklahoma tornado had blown through, leaving the house but destroying everything else.

Lilly wouldn't cry. She couldn't allow herself that pleasure, not when so much needed to be done. She had to think of Shelby, and remain strong for her. And where was that silly puppy? He had to be around somewhere. A sob escaped with a few tears, and all over the puppy.

"We'll get him, Lilly." Ian's hand was on her back as they walked from room to room, stepping over glass and fragments of dishes.

She couldn't tell him that the tears were for that dog he had dumped on them. How could she ever live that down? One look around, and she knew that the tears were for the destruction of the new life she had been trying to build for them. Just stuff, only belongings, but it all symbolized a fresh start. Now it was gone.

"No, we won't, Ian. I'm really starting to doubt that he can be caught. He's evaded the police in two states. He's always here, but never in sight." She glanced toward the window. "He's probably watching right now."

"He isn't going to win."

"He already has. He's stolen my peace."

"Peace is given to us by God. Remember, Jesus promised peace, His peace. Not the world's idea of peace, which is fleeting, but His, which is eternal and not made of worldly things."

"So where is my peace?"

"Ask for it. It's as simple as that."

Lilly walked away from him. He made it sound too easy. If it was so easy . . .

" 'Peace, peace, wonderful peace, coming down from the Father above, sweep over my spirit forever I pray, in fathomless billows of love . . .' " Ian's strong voice sang softly, the words sending shivers up Lilly's spine.

She stopped walking and listened. He sang it again. This time she whispered the words, and as she did, she was surprised by the easing of her mind, and the peace that came to her.

"You win." She turned to face him as he stopped singing. "I have not because I ask not."

"Something like that."

"So, what do I do with this mess?" She swept her arm around, encompassing what remained of the home she had tried to build for her niece.

"We'll get it cleaned up."

"I will."

"Let me help."

Lilly wanted to let him help, but the more she let him into her life, the harder it became to resist him. Sometimes she wondered why she wanted to resist, and that thought scared her more than Carl did.

He took a step toward her. Lilly closed her eyes as his hand touched her face, and then her hair. She felt herself leaning toward him, sensed his face lowering. Their lips touched briefly, gently.

The sharp puppy bark split the air. Lilly jumped back, what remained of her common sense returning to chastise her for her momentary loss of sanity.

"I think we've found the puppy." Ian winked as he walked away, and Lilly's heart melted in a puddle on the floor. Just something else she'd have to clean up.

And she'd better do it soon before the mess grew.

"How long have you been back?" Ian's mother caught Lilly in the kitchen after lunch. She had the look of a mother ready to do battle. That took Lilly by surprise.

"Since September." Lilly set down the pan she had washed.

Before she could say more, Shelby ran into the room carrying a paper airplane. "Hi, sweetie."

"I made it all by myself." She held the plane up for Mrs. Hunt to examine.

"You did, and it is a very fine airplane."

"Go outside and fly it high into the sky, and then it's your nap time." Lilly kissed her niece's cheek. "You're a good girl, Shelby."

Shelby ran from the house, leaving Lilly and Mrs. Hunt alone again. Lilly would have preferred escaping with her niece.

"You hurt him when you left. He never really talked about it, not to me. He's never included me in his life." Mrs. Hunt pulled out the coffee pot and filled it with water. "I believe that he thinks I don't understand him. But I do."

"Of course you do. You're his mother."

"I only want to make it clear that I don't dislike you. I just don't want to see Ian hurt again. And when you leave, he will be hurt."

Mrs. Hunt poured the water into the coffee maker, and filled the filter with coffee. With a stiff parting smile she walked out of the room, leaving Lilly alone with her guilt, and thoughts of leaving again.

But she couldn't escape Elizabeth Hunt's warning. How had she missed it? That her leaving had hurt Ian. They had been friends, nothing more. Or at least she had tried to tell herself that. For a long time she had even believed it.

His proposal that day at the bus station? He had only been offering her a way out of a bad situation. Or had there been more? Lilly pushed the thoughts aside and poured herself a cup of coffee.

Ian hadn't been hurt. Of course he hadn't. He had been too busy having fun back then. He had been busy with college, busy with some girl in a sorority that his mother had set him up with.

At least that was how she had remembered it. Now her memory seemed fuzzy and the details faded, like a worn photo, lacking features and color.

CHAPTER 13

Late the next afternoon Lilly walked across the lawn, the puppy nipping at her heels. She shook her foot at him, but that only encouraged his assault. He made a noise that was probably meant to be a growl and then he shook her pant leg in his puppy teeth. Lilly reached down and picked him up.

Not that she wanted to hold him. She definitely didn't want that. She only wanted to save the hem of her jeans.

Ian walked out of the barn and spotted her heading in his direction. He waved and instead of going back inside, he headed across the parking lot toward her.

The sun glinted on the streaks of blond in his hair, and his smile dazzled in his tanned face.

Someday I'll leave, she reminded her heart. *Don't get too attached.*

"What are you doing out here?" Ian stopped in front of her, windswept brown hair, hazel eyes and a smile that made her want to stay in this spot forever, with horses in the corral behind them, and the sun warming the earth.

No cowboys seemed like a rule that someone else made at some other time, in some other life.

"I wanted to see the new foal you were talking about last night at dinner. And since Shelby is down for a nap, I decided it would be a good time."

"Come this way." He slipped his arm through hers. "She's a beauty."

"You say that about all the girls," Lilly teased.

Ian laughed and pulled her closer to his side. "Only

175

the ones I truly care about."

Lilly ignored the comment. "Are you going to ride this weekend?" She effectively switched the conversation back to him, and his life.

"No. I told you, I'm quitting."

"Sure, of course."

She wanted to believe him, but she knew it wasn't that easy. More than once she had heard her dad make the same promise to her mother. Bull riding was an addiction for some men. It wasn't easy to quit, to walk away from the adrenaline rush, and the excitement.

"I mean it, Lilly. I don't break promises."

"I know you don't." She also didn't want to continue the conversation. "So, where is this foal?"

"She's in here with her mother."

He led her into the stable and she was greeted by the familiar scent of horse, pine shavings and hay. It was a good smell. She breathed deeply, enjoying the warmth, the sounds and the scents.

"Nothing like coming home."

She ignored him. She had enough of her own thoughts without him adding to them. A whinny from the first stall drew her attention. She looked in and saw the pride and joy of Ian's life.

The tiny foal, a black-and-white paint, stood next to his mother. Dark luminous eyes looked up at them, perfect ears twitched, and he stepped forward to be blocked by his mother who wasn't yet willing to let him explore the world on his own.

"He's beautiful."

"Coming from you, that means a lot." Ian leaned on the door and reached to pet the mother's neck.

"What do you mean?"

"Well, horses aren't your favorite animals. Although there is hope, since you're still holding the puppy you said you didn't like. And also, as much as you say you dislike horses, I know that you *know* horses."

"You think you know so much." She held tight to the squirming puppy, who had decided he wanted down to explore.

"You can let him down. He's not going to hurt anything, and he has to learn to behave out here."

She set the puppy down, and he sat at her feet, ears perked and intelligent eyes studying her face. His gray-blue head cocked to one side and his tongue lolled out. He was almost cute. Almost.

"I should be getting back to the house. Your dad was reading a paper and promised to keep an ear out for Shelby."

"He's a good person. They both are. They just have a hard time understanding their only child. I think they've spent a lot of years wishing I'd been a little more like them."

She realized that she was a lot like his parents, always trying to make Ian be who she wanted him to be. He had always supported her dreams. She had always chastised him for his.

"You . . ." She wasn't sure what she should say, especially with him looking at her with questions forming in his eyes. She would rather that he not put those questions into words. He might ask her something like how did she truly feel about him. She didn't want to answer that. "Ian, they should be proud of you, of who you are."

"Was that hard to say?" He smiled, softening the words, and the hurt in his tone.

"Not at all." She looked away, turning her attention back to the foal, who had wandered closer while his mother nibbled at hay. "You do everything as if you're doing it for God. I feel small in comparison."

He moved close to her side, and when she looked up, he was even closer than she had expected. He touched her hair, and his eyes softened.

"Lilly, if you say another word, I'm going to have to kiss you."

"Word," she whispered.

His head lowered, and his lips touched hers. His hand moved to the back of her head and he pulled her closer. She lifted her hand, her fingers coming into contact with his forearms.

The kiss reached down, touching her heart, making her think of things like . . . love. The word sprang to her mind, and she jerked back. The foal skittered across the stall, kicking up straw as he pranced around his mother.

Obviously, this was a good time for Lilly to escape. Before Ian could stop her, she scooped up the puppy and left the barn. As she walked away, she heard his soft chuckle.

If she didn't leave soon . . . if she didn't leave soon . . . She didn't know how to finish that thought.

When Lilly walked into the kitchen, Elizabeth Hunt was there. She smiled up from the cookbook she held in her hands. An apron, looking oddly out of place with her linen dress, was strapped around her waist.

"Do you know if there is any baking soda in this kitchen?" Elizabeth asked.

"Baking soda?"

"For cooking, dear. I plan to cook tonight, if I can remember how." She laughed, a rusty but genuine laugh. "Kathy is with her daughter. I think I can handle it. I used to cook a lot, and then life got busy and I forgot how much I enjoyed it."

Lilly opened the cabinet where the baking soda was kept. She lifted it off the rack and handed it to the other woman. Elizabeth set it on the counter.

"I knew your mother. I guess you probably know that." She didn't look up when she made that statement. She had a measuring spoon in one hand, and the cookbook in the other. "She was a friend of mine. When I left here to go to college, she told me that I would forget all about them, and about who I was."

Lilly didn't know what to say. She wasn't the person to hear the confessions of another woman who had chosen to run as fast and as far as she could from her home, and a life that made her feel trapped.

"I knew that you had been friends." Lilly gave the only answer she felt comfortable with.

"I love my son." Elizabeth set the cookbook down and smiled at Lilly. "I've just felt betrayed by him. He should have used his gift for something great, and he's wasted it."

"It isn't wasted," Lilly defended. "He does great things for the people in this community. Why should a gift only be considered useful if it is used someplace big and prestigious?"

"Because I'm his mother, and mothers always want the biggest and best for their children."

"What about happiness?"

"You love him." Elizabeth Hunt's eyes widened.

"I . . ." What should she say to that?

The back door opened, and Elizabeth turned back to the cookbook. Ian walked through the door of the laundry room into the kitchen. Lilly turned away from his questioning looks, and busied herself by emptying the dishwasher.

"Far too quiet in here." He ran water and filled a glass. "Did I interrupt something?"

"Nothing, dear. Lilly was helping me with dinner."

Ian seemed to notice his mother, the apron and the cookbook for the first time. He set the empty glass on the table and took a step back.

"Mom, do you realize you're wearing an apron?"

She smiled down at the garment and then smiled at her son. "I do know, and I'm going to show you that I haven't lost my touch in the kitchen."

Lilly felt a funny thing, a little like respect, for Elizabeth Hunt. And she realized that it was time to give mother and son time alone together.

"So, you're happy living in Oklahoma?" Ian's dad walked into the barn, looking very out of place in gray dress slacks. It was early evening, and dusk was settling over the valley. Ian switched on a light.

"This is my home, Dad." Ian dumped a scoop of grain into the trough for the mare. The foal edged up next to her and rubbed his whiskered nose against the oats, and then blew, scattering them across the trough.

"Nice horse." His dad stood next to him. "Yes, I guess it is your home. You're a lot like your grandfather. I just hate to see you wasting yourself—your talents—in this place."

Ian walked away, hoping to squelch words that he didn't want to say. Anger tried to boil to the surface, and he knew that if he opened his mouth to defend himself, the anger might bubble to the surface and spill out in words that he couldn't take back. His dad followed him into the stable office, a determined look on his face.

Ian pulled a bottle of water out of the fridge and offered his dad one. David Hunt shook his head. He had already taken the seat behind Ian's desk. His mouth was set in a grim line. Once again, Ian was the recalcitrant teen, out of control, rebelling against the dictates of his parents who "only wanted the best" for him. "The best" had been *their* best, *their* will and *their* plan.

They had never understood, or at least his father hadn't understood, Ian's desire to find God's will for his life. It had been a foreign concept to David Hunt, who had always sought the best career path and nothing more.

"Dad, I think we both know that you didn't come merely for a visit. There's a point to this, to the questions. I'd rather get it out in the open."

"Fine." He took the water and sat down on the old bus seat that served as a couch. "There's a position open in our hospital. We need a good pediatrician. Say the word and the job is yours."

"Head of pediatrics?" Ian sipped from his water. "That's quite an offer. I guess I would be crazy to turn that down."

Lilly stood in the door of the stable, listening to a conversation she had no right to hear. But she had heard, and for some reason, her heart had done a body slam into the wall of her chest.

Ian had the chance to leave, to have a position that most doctors could only dream of. She knew what that meant. It meant watching him walk away. This time she would be the one left in Oklahoma. She turned away from the door, no longer knowing what she wanted to say to Ian, or how to say it.

And how would she say good-bye?

Footsteps in the hallway caught Lilly's attention. She started to freeze, but the booted steps were familiar. She kept reading and waited for Ian to make his presence known.

He stopped at the doorway to the sitting room. Lilly put

her book down on her lap and waited for him to say something. She had avoided his presence for the last two days—since the day she overheard his conversation with his father.

"I'm taking Mom and Dad to the airport. Do you want to ride along?"

"No, I think I'll stay here with Shelby. She wants to play with the puppy, and I don't think she would appreciate a long drive."

"You could leave her with Kathy."

Lilly knew that she could do that, but she didn't want to. Her heart ached with unasked questions, and fears that Ian would leave them. If she went with him, had time alone with him, what would they say to one another? Would she be able to spend time alone and not question him?

But then, wouldn't it be better to ask, to get it out in the open? Of course it would, but she wasn't sure if she wanted to hear his answer.

Had she always loved him, or had it just happened? She couldn't answer that question, because it was one that only her heart knew the answer to. Would he leave, now, just when she was beginning to explore these feelings?

"Lilly, I asked if you would be here when I get back."

"Of course I will. Where would I go?" To her destroyed house? Back to Kansas City? Or off into the sunset?

"I don't want you to leave, not without saying good-bye."

"I understand."

His eyes narrowed, as if he didn't understand. She smiled, hoping to let him know that it was okay. Of course it was okay. She'd never had a broken heart before, but she'd heard that time heals all wounds.

After watching Ian drive away with his parents, Lilly went in search of Kathy and Shelby. She found the two of them in the back yard collecting fall leaves that had dropped to the ground.

"Shelby, how about a trip to town? I need to pick a few things up at the store."

Shelby stuffed a few more leaves into her bag. "Okay, Aunt Lilly. But can I take Dolly?"

The new doll that Ian had brought home for her a few days ago. She had hardly put the thing down in that time. It surprised Lilly that the doll wasn't with the little girl at that moment.

"Of course you can take your doll. I'm going to find my purse." She smiled at Kathy, who had an armload of leaves. "Do you want to go? Or do you need anything?"

"Not a thing. Oh, wait. I could use cocoa powder. And you could tell me why you're wearing such a long face."

"I'll get the cocoa, and my face isn't long." She tried a smile but it felt out of place. Ian was leaving them. Lilly didn't plan on being the one to tell.

On the drive into town, Lilly thought about what the future held for her. She had planned on staying in Oklahoma. She wanted to raise Shelby near Kathy, Jamie, and Johnny. She had wanted Ian in their lives. Now, if Ian left, where did that leave them? What happened next?

What about God's plan? The thought came unbidden, forcing her to think beyond the here and now. What about it? She wanted to yell into the wind, to demand answers. She really, truly wanted God's perfect plan, but how did she find it?

She had to talk to Ian. She had to know what was on his mind, and in his heart. That decision made, she felt a sense of relief wash over her. As soon as Ian got home, she would talk to him and find out what his plans were.

"Aunt Lilly, I have to go to the bathroom."

They had been on the road for fifteen minutes. Tulsa was still thirty minutes away. Lilly glanced in the rearview mirror and smiled at her squirming niece. It appeared the stop couldn't be put off.

"Okay, I'll stop at the next convenience store."

And lucky for them, she saw one just up the road. She took the exit and pulled up to the building. Shelby had her seatbelt off the minute the van stopped.

"Bad, huh?"

Shelby nodded, "Real bad."

Lilly took her niece by the hand and led her into the convenience store. The bathrooms were in the back corner. The way Shelby was dancing next to her, it was probably a good thing that they hadn't needed to drive farther to find a place to stop.

"Before we leave here, we'll get snacks," Lilly offered as she opened the door to the restroom.

Shelby ignored her, and pushed into the empty restroom stall.

"Okay, I get the point. We'll talk about snacks when you get done." Lilly pulled lipstick from her purse and applied a thin coat while she waited.

"Can I have chocolate?" Shelby asked when she walked up to the sink.

"Wash your hands and we'll discuss it when we get out there."

They walked through the suddenly crowded convenience store. Every traveler on the interstate must have decided it was time for a break. Lilly led Shelby through a group of teenagers gathered around the deli.

"How about a sandwich, and if you eat that, you can have chocolate?" Lilly held tight to Shelby's hand. The little girl kept trying to pull away from her, lured by the sight of brightly colored candy wrappers two aisles away.

"Can I go pick out my candy?"

Lilly glanced around the store. There was a group of teenagers beside her, and a couple at the counter buying coffee. It seemed safe. The candy was only ten feet away. Lilly didn't want to be paranoid. She didn't want Shelby to grow up always looking over her shoulder.

"Go ahead, but don't wander away. Get your candy and come right back to me."

Shelby grinned broadly and skipped away. Lilly watched her, and then turned back to the deli counter when the worker asked what she needed.

The girl at the counter took Lilly's order for two ham sandwiches, no mayo on one. When she turned back to ask Shelby if she wanted apple juice, the little girl had disappeared.

"Shelby, come here and let me know what you want to drink."

She moved away from the deli, hoping she would find Shelby on the next aisle. There was no sign of her. White-hot panic flashed through her body. Hot and cold all at once, Lilly fought against the fear. She had to stay calm. She had to be logical. Shelby had been there just moments ago. She couldn't have gone anywhere. Lilly would have known.

"Shelby?" she called out louder. The deli girl gave her a look. The teenagers shook their heads and walked away. "Shelby?"

Lilly ran up to the cashier at the counter. "My niece, did you see her? The little girl that came in with me."

The cashier shrugged her shoulders as she counted change back to the man paying for a gallon of milk. Both of them looked at her as if she had gone crazy.

"No, I didn't see a little girl."

Lilly leaned over the counter, forcing the woman to pay attention to her. The man picked up his milk and walked out, mumbling about a crazy female. Lilly didn't care. If she had to be crazy to get their attention, she would.

"She had blond curls. I brought her in with me a few minutes ago."

"Oh, yeah, her daddy came in here and got her. He said it was a surprise and not to tell you."

"No, no. Please call the police." Lilly fought back the tears. She had to stay calm. "Please call nine-one-one."

She ran outside, hoping she wouldn't be too late, hoping that the car was still in the parking lot. It was too late, though. And it was her fault. She had let her guard down. Because of her, Carl had Shelby, and she might never see her again.

A sharp pain jabbed at her heart. She had let Shelby down. And once again, she had let Missy down.

A blur of activity buzzed around Lilly as she sat on the curb outside the store. Police cars arrived, lights flashing and sirens blaring. The officers asked questions, and numbly she gave the answers. She shook her head when they asked if there was anyone they could call for her.

She had no one. Not really. They could call Kathy, but Kathy didn't have a car. Ian was with his parents. And she had to stop relying on Ian.

Someone pushed a cup of coffee into her hand. She took it and sipped. It didn't really taste of anything. The hot liquid slid down her throat and she closed her eyes. If only this could be a dream.

"Ma'am, we would like to take you to the station."

Lilly looked up, surprised by the voice, by the statement. "The station. But I didn't do anything."

"No, ma'am, that isn't the reason. You can't stay here. We're searching the area, but, well . . ."

She nodded her understanding. "I can't stay here until they find her." She choked on a sob. "What if they don't find her? What if she comes back and I'm not here?"

"We'll do our best."

Lilly pushed herself up from the curb where she had been sitting for a long time. She didn't know how long, but long enough for her legs to cramp. The coffee cup was empty, and several of the police cars had left.

"I should go look for her." She reached into her purse for her keys. "I want to go find her."

"Ma'am, we can't let you drive in this condition. We have cars all over the state looking for her."

Numb with pain, Lilly nodded in response to what seemed a logical explanation. She allowed the officer to lead her to a car. She was grateful that he opened the front passenger door, not the back. She couldn't take that, not now, when she felt like she was the one to blame . . . the guilty one.

The police station was in a small community just a few miles from the convenience store. Lilly followed the officer into the building to a small room with a few chairs and a desk.

"The chief said to let you sit in here," Officer Jones—she read on his nametag—explained. "I'll get you a Coke or something."

"Nothing, thank you." Her stomach rolled at the idea of putting anything inside her body. She stared at the chairs, and then out the window. A storm was blowing up, big dark clouds and wind that swirled the tops of the trees in circles.

"I'll be back." Officer Jones backed out of the room, his expression full of sympathy. Lilly nodded, wanting him to go. She needed to be alone. Closing her eyes she felt a strong urge to pray. She couldn't take care of Shelby. She couldn't be strong enough. God was there, sheltering them from the storm.

CHAPTER 14

Ian followed Dean through the police station to a room at the back of the building. Through the open door he could see Lilly sitting in a chair next to the window, her head resting on the arm that she had draped over the armrest.

Dean motioned him forward. "I'll be back in a few minutes."

Lilly didn't move, not at first. Ian considered that she might be sleeping, but as he drew nearer, her gaze came up to meet his. Her tear-streaked face and the tangle of brown hair took him back in time. Only now the girl was a woman, and he knew that the feelings she stirred in him were stronger than a crush, stronger than physical attraction. He loved her.

"Ian." She sobbed on his name. "She's gone. He took her."

"I know." He crossed the room and sat in the chair next to hers. He touched her hand, rubbing gently across the tops of her fingers. "I'm sorry, Lil. But we'll find them."

"I'm so afraid." She looked away, out the window at the storm that raged, turning the afternoon dark and ominous.

"It's okay to be afraid." He wrapped his hand around hers. "But we have to trust that God is in control. He'll get us through this."

"I know, but I'm not sure if I can be strong right now. I keep trying to find faith, but I feel like I'm drifting and I'm alone."

"You aren't alone. God is here. He sent me. We're going

to make it through this, and we're going to get her back."

"I feel so weak, Ian. I'm so tired of being strong. I'm so tired of trying to find my way."

"Let me help you, Lilly. That doesn't mean you stop being strong. It just means that we can be strong together."

"How did you know?"

"Dean was on duty when they issued the Amber Alert."

"Tell him thank you. I really didn't want to bother you, not now with everything going on in your life." She smiled up at him. "But I'm glad you're here."

Ian released her hand. He sat back in the chair and tried to tell himself not to be hurt. "Lilly, why do you think you have to handle everything alone? Don't you realize that we care about you, and you can count on us? On me?"

She nodded and on her own she reached for his hand, "I'm sorry. I didn't mean to hurt you."

"I know."

"Ian, I can't sit here and do nothing. I need to go out and search. I need to find Shelby."

"I don't think that's a good idea. The police are searching."

"Please, don't make me do this alone."

Ian stood up, still holding her hand. Her fingers grasped his and he pulled her to her feet. "I'll help you find her."

Dean met them in the hall. "Where are you going?"

"We're going to help search. We can't sit here and do nothing."

"I understand. If I hear anything, I'll call."

"Thanks, Dean."

They walked outside, into forty-mile-per-hour wind gusts and pelting rain. Ian wrapped an arm around Lilly's waist and pulled her toward his truck. Once they were inside, he reached into the console between the seats and pulled out a pile of napkins. He handed her one and she wiped the water off her face.

"I'm glad you're here." She smiled tremulously and a tear trickled down her cheek.

"I wouldn't be anywhere else."

And once they found Shelby, he feared he would face losing them all over again. For now he had to concentrate on finding her, on bringing her back to Lilly.

Lilly leaned her forehead against the truck window and stared into the dimming light of early evening. She sighed, thinking for a moment that it was hopeless. Carl could be anywhere, and how would she see him? How could she find him in the dark?

How would she find him at night, when for weeks he had evaded them in the daylight? She closed her eyes, praying silently for God's help, and for those mercies of His.

Ian pulled a light out of the console between them and plugged it into the power source. He handed it to her, with an accompanying smile.

"It's a spotlight," he explained. "Turn it on, and flash it into the fields and the ditches. If he's out there, we're going to find him."

Lilly took the light and flipped the switch as she pointed it out into the field. It felt better, doing something. She needed to fill her time, not sit and do nothing while others hunted.

Mile after mile they drove, past farms, subdivisions, and small communities. They checked hotel parking lots, side streets and restaurants. The hope Lilly had felt ebbed as the hours ticked by.

Ian remained silent, except for the prayers he sometimes whispered. She knew that he was holding on to the slim thread of hope that dangled in front of him.

She held on to his faith, his hope, knowing it would have to get her through for now. In a way it became her own, because she believed that if Ian prayed, if Ian had faith, that everything would be okay, and that they would survive this.

"I need coffee, Lilly." His voice sounded strained, tired. Lilly flipped off the light and turned away from the window.

Ian sat hunched over the steering wheel, his shoulders stiff, tense lines around his mouth. She glanced at the clock. It was nearly three in the morning. He had been driving for hours. Lilly leaned back against the seat and sighed.

"I'm so sorry, Ian. I haven't paid attention. I didn't realize we'd been out here so long."

"You don't have to be sorry." He flipped on the turn signal and slowed as they approached an all-night diner just off the interstate. "We'll go in here, get a bite to eat and show them Shelby's picture."

"Good idea."

Ian pulled into a parking space. He hugged the steering wheel, and Lilly scooted closer so that she could reach him. She rubbed between his shoulders and he turned, giving her better access. She massaged, kneading the tense muscles until they started to relax.

"Thank you," he whispered.

"You're the best friend a person could have, Ian." She leaned on his shoulder. "Sometimes that's the best place to start, with a friendship."

"Don't say things in a moment of crisis," he warned. "I'm not holding out for a big change in your feelings, so let's not say things that you might regret. Right now the important thing is finding Shelby."

"You're right, and I'm sorry. I can't imagine going

through this without you." She leaned her forehead on his shoulder. "But then, you've seen me through every major crisis of my life."

"No, Lilly, you've seen yourself through. I helped, but I didn't make you survive."

She touched his arm before moving away. "In some ways you're right. But you've always been there for me, and I appreciate that."

She grabbed her purse and reached for her door handle, but she didn't open it. She had one last thing to tell him, something she couldn't put off. If he left, then at least he would leave knowing how his friendship had changed her.

"Ian, thank you for showing me that I can trust a cowboy. You'll never know how much you mean to me."

She didn't look back to see how he reacted to her words. It didn't matter. The only thing that really mattered was getting Shelby back.

"I'm going to call the police while we're here," Ian told her after he'd ordered an omelet and a cup of coffee. "Why don't you show the picture to the waitress and the hostess, see if they recognize Shelby?"

"I will."

Ian stepped outside into the cool, rain-dampened night air. He dialed his house and watched through the window as Lilly walked through the restaurant showing Shelby's picture. With each "no" answer she received, he could see her shoulders drooping as discouragement weighed down on her.

"Hello, Ian, is that you?" Kathy's voice shook him from his thoughts.

"Yes, it's me. Have you heard anything?"

"Not since the last time you called. Come home, Ian.

The two of you need to rest."

"We will rest, but we can't leave. We'll probably head back to the police station and wait there."

"You be careful out there."

"Get some sleep, Kathy. I'll call you if we hear anything."

Ian dropped the phone into his pocket and walked back into the diner. Lilly was in their booth, her head cradled in her hands. He scooted in next to her and wrapped an arm around her shoulder. She shivered beneath his touch, and he rubbed the cold skin of her arm.

"I'll buy you a jacket at the truck stop before we leave here." He pulled her close, offering what warmth he could.

"You don't have to. I'm fine."

"No, you're not fine, Lilly. You've always said that, and you've always tried to make it true, but this time it isn't true. You're afraid, you're tired and you're cold. We're going to eat something, have a cup of coffee and then we're going in for awhile so we can both rest."

"But I . . ."

"You won't do Shelby any good if you're sick."

She bent her head over the cup of coffee that she held between her two hands, and her hair fell forward, hiding her expression from view. Ian brushed her thick wave of hair back so that he could see her face.

"Lilly, she's going to come home."

"I can't take this, Ian. I can't take the fear, or the constant flow of tears. Just when I think it's over, the tears start again."

"It's okay to cry."

"Tears won't bring her home."

"No, but prayers can." He didn't want that to be a trite response to her fears. Prayer could work. They had to trust in God. Better to trust in God and His plan than in themselves.

He moved to the other side of the booth. The waitress arrived with two plates, and the glass carafe to refill their coffee cups.

She offered them a sympathetic smile, set their plates in front of them and then refilled their cups.

"Here you go, kids. I just want you all to know that we'll keep an eye out for that little girl. And we'll sure be praying for you."

Lilly touched the woman's arm. "Thank you for that."

The waitress nodded, patted Lilly's shoulder and walked away. Lilly spooned more sugar into her coffee, and then pushed the sugar bowl in his direction. Ian slid it to the back of the table.

"I haven't prayed this much in years," she admitted. "Do you think God allowed this to happen on purpose, to bring me to this point?"

"God isn't punishing you, Lilly." Ian pushed his hand through his hair, praying he would have the right answer for her. "I know that circumstances can bring us back to God. We're in the middle of something traumatic, and we realize that we need faith to get through. I don't think that necessarily means that God allowed it to happen. I don't think your faith is in question."

"I think I agree, but right now it just feels like life is playing a dirty trick on me."

"But God isn't," Ian reminded. He pointed to her omelet. "Eat. You need to have something in your stomach besides coffee."

Ian finished his omelet, another cup of coffee, and then he laid a twenty on the table to cover the bill. "Let's go back to the station and see how things are going."

She took his hand and they walked out the door together. Ian opened the passenger door and Lilly climbed in.

195

She stopped him from closing the door.

"You deserve everything, Ian. You deserve someone who appreciates you, someone who is willing to be the wife you want."

"Not right now, Lilly. It isn't the time or the place for this conversation." He didn't want to hear it, not tonight. He was too old for the "you're a nice guy, but . . ." discussion.

They drove to the station in silence, arriving as the sky in the east was turning a lighter gray. Patrol cars were pulling in, their shift over for the day. Other cars pulled in to the parking lot as the new crew arrived.

Ian glanced across the cab to Lilly. She had already fallen asleep. It wasn't a sound sleep. She moved fitfully and seemed to be talking. If he woke her up, would she go back to sleep? She would probably sleep more soundly in his truck than in a chair in the police station. Rather than waking her up, he reached into the backseat of the truck for the blanket he kept there. He placed it over her shoulders, watching to make sure it didn't wake her.

Cool fall air brushed across Ian's face as he stepped out of the truck. He stretched, relieving the kinks in his arms and back. A door opened at the front of the station and Dean walked across the parking lot.

"What are you still doing here?" Ian lowered his voice, glancing into the truck to make sure he hadn't woken Lilly.

"The sheriff let me stay on last night."

"You're a good friend, Dean."

"You'd do the same for me."

They crossed the parking lot together. "So, nothing new?"

Dean shook his head, "Nothing."

Ian felt his hope deflate. The more time that passed, the harder this became. He hated feeling useless.

"We'll find her," Dean assured him.

Ian didn't answer. He followed his friend into the police station. A pot of coffee was brewing. They waited for it to finish and then poured themselves each a cup.

"I'm going to let Lilly sleep for awhile. When she wakes up, she'll want to start searching again."

"You need some sleep, too."

"Yeah, but I needed out of that truck for a few hours more than I needed sleep." He normally drank his coffee black, but this stuff was stronger than mud. He poured a spoon of creamer in and it turned to light gray mud. "You need sleep, too."

Dean shrugged. "I can take it."

Ian finished the coffee and tossed the cup into the trash. "I'm going back out to the truck. We'll be here for awhile, so let me know if you hear anything."

A kink in her neck woke Lilly up. She blinked against bright morning sun that filtered through the window of the truck, stretched the kinks from her legs, and then glanced toward the driver's side. Ian slept, head against the rolled-up window of the door, and his legs over the center console.

"Ian, it's morning," she whispered, touching his arm.

"I know," he mumbled, rubbing his face before opening his eyes. "I wasn't sleeping."

She almost smiled, and then she remembered. Shelby was gone. Carl had her out there somewhere. She would be frightened, maybe worried. And what if she was in danger?

Early morning sunshine couldn't dispel the bleakness in Lilly's heart at that moment. Ian seemed to understand. He sat up and reached across the cab of the truck for her hand.

"Let's pray," he spoke softly, as his eyes filled with tears.

Ian crying. She couldn't handle that. He had to be the

197

strong one. He was always strong. For once she couldn't—
she just couldn't—be that person, the one holding it all together.

"I just wanted to wake up and have this all be some horrible dream," she admitted.

"I know," Ian sighed and brushed at the few tears that
trickled down his face. "We need to pray, Lilly. Right now,
we need to pray."

She nodded, bowed her head and closed her eyes as Ian
prayed. She remembered him singing to her about peace,
and as he prayed, she felt that same peace descending. She
kept her eyes closed, even after Ian's final amen. She wanted
to stay there, in that place of peace, in God's presence.

Ian released her hand and she looked up, still awash in
the sweet spirit that had invaded the cab of the truck.

"Ian, I felt God. It was so real, so awesome. I want to
stay here with Him."

"He's going where you're going, Lilly. He always has."

God had always been with her. She believed that. She
could even think of times when she had felt so alone, and
yet not alone. She could remember times when a need had
been met, or a question answered. God had never left her
alone.

And He wouldn't leave Shelby alone.

"Do you want to search again?"

She nodded, "If you don't mind. I can't just sit here."

"Let's search in the direction of home." He turned to
look at her. "Lilly, we can't stay here forever. We have to go
home. And when they find her, they'll bring her there."

"What if . . ." She stopped herself from saying words she
didn't want to think. "What if she needs me and I'm not
here."

"You'll be there for her."

Home. She no longer knew what that word meant, or how to get there. She did know one thing: she wanted the comfort of Kathy's and Johnny's arms. She wanted Ian at her side.

"Okay, home. Do they know how to contact us?"

"They know. Dean is still here."

Lilly nodded—she couldn't say the words—that they could leave. She couldn't verbalize her thoughts, her fears, that Shelby might return to the convenience store looking for her and she wouldn't be there.

Ian pulled the truck into his drive. He pushed the remote opener for the garage and eased into his normal parking spot.

"We're here." He touched Lilly's arm and she opened her eyes.

"I fell asleep." She covered a yawn with her hand. "I should have stayed awake. I could have been watching."

"You have to sleep. You can't stop taking care of yourself."

A storm brewed in her eyes and then passed on. "I know that. But I can't stop looking."

"We won't stop, Lilly. But we do need to get cleaned up, change clothes and rest for awhile."

Personally, he wanted to shave and change out of the shirt he'd had on for two days. At this point he couldn't be pleasant to be around, not with hat hair and the start of a beard.

"Ian, thank you for putting up with me."

He hadn't expected that.

"You're welcome, Lilly. But I haven't been 'putting up' with you. You need to accept that friends help each other."

"I know they do. I also know that this has taken you

199

away from work, and away from what you need to be doing here."

"It's covered." The door opened and he glanced up, smiling in Kathy's direction. "Come on, I bet Kathy has something special fixed."

Lilly climbed over the console and slid to the ground next to him. He put a hand on the small of her back and followed her into the house. He smiled for her benefit, but smiling was becoming more difficult. The longer Shelby was gone, the more worried he became. He wanted her back. He wanted her dad behind bars.

"Could we please go look again?" Lilly paced across the living room, avoiding the sympathetic looks of Kathy and Johnny. She focused on Ian.

"No, Lilly, we can't. The police would like for us to stay here, in case they need us."

"Don't say it like that, like we're going to get bad news." She rested her forehead against the cool glass, knowing that nobody would hold her accountable for her outburst, but feeling a lot of guilt for lashing out at people who cared about her.

It had been a long day. Now the sky was turning gray as a second night without Shelby descended. Lilly had forever disliked the short days of winter, when dark came early and seemed to last so long. It left her feeling panicked, and in need of sunlight. Tonight that feeling magnified inside of her.

Ian touched her shoulder. She didn't turn to face him, not with the guilt she was feeling. They'd all been so good to her. She would never be able to repay them for all they'd done.

"I'm sorry. I shouldn't be taking this out on all of you."

"Come and sit down, Lilly. Kathy's fixing you a sandwich, and you need to eat."

She nodded and followed him back to the sofa. The sandwich that Kathy gave her was probably good, but in her mouth it tasted like sawdust. She rinsed it down with the ice water that Ian handed her.

Somehow she managed to eat most of it. And she did feel better, less shaky, and less angry. She sat back, closing her eyes and wondering if maybe she could go to sleep and wake up to find everything normal again.

Johnny turned on the television, and then turned it off again when they saw the Amber Alert flash across the screen with a picture of Shelby. Earlier in the day a reporter from a television station had called, asking for more details, but the details had felt more like a quest for gossip than for news, and Lilly had hung up on the man.

"They'll find her," she whispered.

She looked around the room, at Johnny in the recliner, Kathy in a rocking chair, knitting, and Ian next to her. They all smiled and agreed. Lilly wondered if someday she would still be saying it, that they would find Shelby, and they would stop agreeing.

And how would she face her sister? Guilt again flooded her heart as she thought about Missy in prison, unable to do anything, or even to be comforted by friends or family. Shelby belonged to Missy, her flesh and blood, and she didn't have the option of looking for her.

"What are you thinking about?" Ian touched her hand and she opened her eyes to meet his concerned gaze.

"I'm thinking about Missy, and how she feels right now. She's alone, with no one to hold her hand."

"They've sent a minister to sit with her." He rubbed his jaw, and then exhaled sharply. "I know that doesn't help

201

you to feel better. But it will help her, not to be alone, and to have someone there with her."

"I know." Lilly stood up, no longer able to sit and do nothing. "I know we can't go out and search, but I need to do something. I want to walk. Or drive down to the house. I need to look, to see if I can find something that will show us what Carl has been doing."

"I'll drive you down."

Lilly nodded as she slipped her feet into her sandals. "I appreciate this, Ian. I know you have things you could be doing."

"Those things can wait."

Lilly felt invisible strings attaching them together, and a bond growing that previously had been a thin thread that connected their lives. What would she do without him? She couldn't think about that. Or about how she would feel if he went to Boston, to a job that would take him far from them all.

All those years, telling herself to be strong, and not to rely on someone else to take care of her. In the end a cowboy had broken her heart, just not the way she had always thought it would happen.

CHAPTER 15

The desecrated house sitting in the valley painted a bleak picture. Ian knew that Lilly had to be feeling the same thing. Her fresh start had taken a drastic turn. First, the house she had spent days working on had been destroyed in a matter of hours, and left in worse condition than when she'd moved back.

And Shelby was gone. The mere thought brought an ache to his heart. He could picture the child sitting under the tree next to the house, the puppy napping in her lap.

Where was she now? Had Carl hurt her? Would she be found? They had no answers for those questions. Ian still had his faith.

"Let's walk down through that stand of trees by the creek," he suggested as they walked through the yard. "I've looked there, but always at night with a flashlight."

"It's almost dark now." Lilly looked up at the gray, overcast sky.

"But it's still light enough to look around."

He led her down a path, knowing that she followed close on his heels. As they drew closer to the thick stand of trees he could hear the spring trickling along the rocks. It didn't go far, and normally had a strong flow only after a good rain.

"Ian, I overheard your conversation with your dad."

The words came out of nowhere, taking him by surprise. Ian stopped at the edge of the woods and turned to face the woman who stood behind him, her hands shoved into her pockets.

"You heard what conversation?"

"In the stable. He told you about a job in Boston."

"I see. So, what do you want me to say?"

She shrugged, and averted her eyes to look around them, the woods suddenly holding her interest. "You don't owe me explanations. You wouldn't be the first person to leave home for something better. Or something you thought would be better. I mean, after all, I'll probably go back to Kansas City. They told me I'd always have a job there."

"Lilly . . ."

"Ian, what's that?" She pointed to a tree just a few feet away. The conversation about his move and jobs in Kansas City ended as they both looked up.

"A deer stand. Hunters use them during deer season." Ian touched the boards that had been nailed to the tree in a makeshift ladder. "This one is old, and pretty rough. Your dad probably put it there years ago."

"Ian, someone has been here." She had climbed the first few rungs and was peeking over the edge of the platform that looked like a small tree house. "There are candy wrappers."

Ian climbed up next to her. "Now we know where he was hiding." He looked up. "He could have been hiding here, watching your house. When I came to search he probably climbed higher into the tree. And he kept his car on the back side of the field for a quick escape."

"He was here all along, watching." She shivered as she said the words. "He watched as Shelby played outside. He knew when we were gone."

"I'm sorry, Lil. I should have done more. I should have caught him."

"It isn't your fault." She dropped back to the ground and turned to face him. "You've done more than your share, trying to keep us safe."

"I only wish I could have done more."

She rested her cheek against his shoulder. "Ian, you've done everything possible."

He led her out of the woods and back to his truck. Her hand tightened around his. When he looked down he saw tears glistening on her cheeks. He hadn't done everything possible. He hadn't kept them safe. Her belief in him, that he'd done everything possible, seemed a hollow victory.

Darkness closed in on Ian's house, leaving it in shadows and glowing with warm lamplight. Lilly stood at the window, feeling a warm peace invading her soul. It felt as if God's comforting arms had been wrapped around her, and He whispered into her heart that He had it all in control.

She believed him. Somehow, some way, Shelby would come home to them.

"What are you thinking about?" Ian stood next to her, his hand pulling the cord that raised the wooden blinds on the windows to their highest level.

"God is in control. I know that, and I've always known. But at times like this, when you feel that you're not alone, and you have a peace that seems unexplainable, that's when you really know that it isn't in our hands."

"I agree. I start to worry, to fear, but then the calm re-turns." He leaned his shoulder against hers and she rested her head on his arm. "Take a nap, Lilly."

"I think I'll try."

Sleep had really been the furthest thing from her mind, but somehow it happened. She dozed off, into a dreamless sleep, devoid of nightmares or fear.

A loud pounding on the front door jerked her back to the present. She sat up, realizing that the warm body next to her was Ian's. He squeezed her hand and left her sitting alone on the couch. With sleep-blurred eyes she watched as he walked to the door.

It seemed as if everything went in slow motion. Ian was at the door. Dean was smiling. Even without hearing their words, Lilly knew.

"They found her." Ian's words made it real. Lilly couldn't stop the engulfing wave of emotion that flooded her, bringing with it a downpour of tears. She was up, and Kathy was there, hugging her.

"She's coming home," Kathy cried, "our girl is coming home."

Ian made it to her in only a few steps, hugging her tight, holding her off the ground and spinning her. He kissed her cheek and she held on to him.

"They found them sleeping in his car," Dean explained. "Carl is in custody. We'll be pressing charges here in Oklahoma, and then he'll still face the charges in Missouri. Shelby is with a family services caseworker and a female officer . . . they'll be here in an hour."

Lilly sat down on the sofa, suddenly weak, as all of the adrenaline that had kept her going drained from her body. Shelby would be home in an hour. The ordeal that had started weeks ago when Carl escaped from police custody would finally be over.

They could go on with their lives. She could decide what that meant later. For now it was enough that Shelby was coming home. She looked up, meeting Ian's gaze. The warmth in his glance when he smiled touched her heart as deeply as a physical touch might have.

When car doors slammed less than an hour later, Lilly felt her heart jump into her throat. She hurried to the front door, tears cascading down her cheeks when she saw Shelby step out of the backseat of the car, a ponytailed caseworker holding her hand.

Lilly threw the door open and hurried outside. Shelby broke loose from the hand that held hers and ran up the walk. Lilly pulled the little girl into her arms and held her tight.

She wouldn't let her down again. Somehow she would keep her safe. Shelby would have a life that didn't include the fear of being left alone. Shelby would always have someone to help her through the difficult times. She wouldn't have to do it all alone.

Those were promises Lilly made to herself. She would keep her niece safe. She wouldn't fail again.

Ian forced himself to stand in the background when Shelby walked through the door. He knew that she needed Lilly, and she needed time to settle in. His instinct, to take control and to protect, was firmly in check. It wasn't easy, but it was necessary.

He watched as Lilly held Shelby close, touching her hair, looking into her eyes as she asked if she was okay, and then hugging her again. He wanted to hug them both. He longed to be a part of the homecoming, to share the moment with them rather than sitting back and playing the part of bystander.

After a few minutes they joined him in the living room, where he waited with Kathy and Johnny. Shelby's bottom lip trembled when she tried to smile. Ian could see that if she cried he'd have a room full of tears, including his own.

He kneeled down in front of her.

"Hey, kitten, I sure missed you." He wanted to say more, to tell her how wrong it was for her own father to take her that way. He wanted to promise to protect her. He didn't have that right.

"I missed you, too." Her lip quivered and then she wrapped little arms around his neck and hugged tight.

"You're safe now," he assured her. He stood up and backed into a chair where he could hold her. "We love you."

"I love you, too." She put her head on his shoulder and he rubbed her back.

He sat with her in his lap for several minutes. Then Lilly moved, catching his attention. She put her finger to her lip and stood up. He relinquished control when Lilly pulled the sleeping child from his arms.

Lilly watched Shelby sleeping in her own bed, the stuffed animal curled up under her chin, and the puppy at her feet. The puppy was there because Ian said it could be a house dog for now. Lilly sat down on the edge of the bed, and reached out to smooth the wispy blond hair from Shelby's face.

"I love you," she whispered as she brushed away the few tears that had squeezed out to trickle down her cheeks.

"She loves you, too." Ian walked up behind her and rested his hands on her shoulders. He rubbed gently and she leaned forward.

"I can't believe he did this to her."

"He's behind bars, Lilly. He won't hurt her again." Ian's hands on her shoulders stilled. She glanced back and saw the anger tensing the smiling lines of his mouth.

"I'm not sure what to do now," she admitted. "The danger is over. I need to move forward with our lives."

"I know." He leaned, kissed the top of her head and walked to the bedroom door. "If it makes any difference, I don't want you to go."

It did make a difference. It made it harder for her to

make a decision. And it brought up other questions. Like what about his decision to take a job in Boston. Questions buzzed through her mind but he was gone.

Not that she would have asked.

She looked out at the inky black sky of early November. A star, far to the north, winked in the velvety darkness. Lilly closed her eyes and said a prayer, that God would help her to make the right decision.

Jamie stopped by the next afternoon with the baby. Lilly greeted her at the door, glad to have someone to talk to. Kathy and Johnny were in town. After a morning of riding the pony, Shelby had fallen asleep right after lunch. Ian had been called to the hospital.

"Where is everyone?" Jamie handed Lilly the baby as she rummaged through the fridge. Not only was Jamie company, someone to talk to, but she had brought a moment of normality to the house.

Lilly sat down at the kitchen table, the baby in her arms. She leaned to kiss the soft, rose-petal cheek of the infant. Jamie pulled out chicken salad and turned to smile at them. Her look turned to adoration when it lingered on her child.

"I no longer exist, not since I had that baby. I'm no longer Jamie. Instead I'm *the baby's mom*. I asked you a question."

Lilly had heard, but truth be told, Jamie had been right. Lilly was enthralled by the baby, her coo, the way she drooled, and the smell of baby powder. Jamie was great, but she couldn't compare with a cooing baby whose pudgy baby hands were pinching Lilly's chin.

"I heard you. I just ignored you for a moment. Your parents are shopping. Shelby's sleeping. Ian is at the hospital. He called and he should be home in an hour."

"Is this home?" Jamie sat down across from her with two

glasses of tea. She pushed one glass across the table to Lilly.

"It's Ian's home." Lilly wasn't about to get pulled into a game of words. She would also prefer to ignore the point that Jamie had so effectively made with that question.

"He built it thinking that someday he would get married and, let's see, how did he say it . . . fill it up with kids."

"He's such an optimist." The baby started to fuss and Lilly handed her back to Jamie. "Someday he'll find someone."

Jamie looked up and shook her head. "You are the most contrary female I've ever met."

"And you learned that phrase from your dad. I resent that you're using the term on me that he uses on stubborn horses and noncompliant cows." Lilly finished the tea. "Do you want another glass?"

"Have you eaten today?" Jamie asked.

"I had something," she stopped, and sighed. "I don't re-member what or when."

"Fix yourself something to eat, or take the baby and I'll fix you something."

"No, I'm fine." She walked to the door that led to the deck. "I have a lot on my mind."

"Stop making it so hard, Lil. It isn't that difficult. Stay or go. You came here looking for a place to raise Shelby. Has it stopped being the right place? Do you think God changes His mind so easily? If He directed you here, do you think He now has a different plan?"

More logic. Lilly wasn't in the mood for such sound ad-vice—not when it seemed so simple the way Jamie put it.

"No, God didn't change His plan. It's more complicated than it should be."

"No, it isn't. You're making it complicated because you're stubborn."

Lilly returned to the island. She sat down and picked up

the glass that now held only a few pieces of melting ice. She swirled them until Jamie took the glass from her hand.

"I'm not stubborn," she admitted. "I'm afraid."

"Of Ian?" Jamie laughed. "That's the most ridiculous thing I've ever heard. I could see you being afraid of . . . other things. Be afraid of spiders, of mice, and maybe of the dark. But not Ian."

"It's not Ian that I'm afraid of." She reached for the glass and sipped the last of its contents. "I know you're going to be amazed by this, but I'm afraid of losing him."

Jamie sighed, "You don't want him to die on a bull. You don't want to be let down, the way your father let your mother down. Lilly, we all understand, but come on, you know that Ian is his own person and that you can trust him to make right decisions."

That hurt. It was true, but it hurt. Or maybe it used to be true, back in the days when she wanted all cowboys in the same small box. Ian didn't fit the mold.

And the stakes had changed. Now it wasn't a bull she was afraid of, it was the idea of him walking away from all of them. And as soon as he got back from town, she planned on finding out what he planned to do.

"Ian isn't your dad, Lil."

"I know that. This time there is more going on than I can tell you."

"Like what?"

"That's for Ian to answer. But I plan on finding out for myself as soon as he gets home."

"Are you going to Kansas City to work?"

"I'm not planning to. Not if I can get a job here."

Lilly got up to refill her tea glass. She pulled the pitcher out of the fridge and held it up to Jamie.

"Do you want more?"

Jamie shook her head. "I've had enough caffeine for the day."

Lilly poured herself a glass of tea and moved back to her chair. "As much as I want to stay, though, do you think this is the right place for Shelby? I'm new at this 'mom' business. Will she be able to be happy here? Or do we need to start somewhere new, where she won't have to deal with memories of what her dad did to her?"

"I'm sort of new to the 'mom' business myself." Jamie picked up Lilly's glass of tea and took a long drink. "But kids are resilient. They have a way of healing, and of moving on. We're the ones who get stuck in the past."

Lilly looked out the window, focusing on the blue of the Oklahoma sky. It looked as if it should be warm out, but it wasn't. Fall had definitely descended with crisp weather and clear skies.

"What if Ian were to leave?" Lilly hadn't meant to say the words out loud, but she did, and Jamie grabbed hold of the topic.

"Ian, leave here? Leave his job, his horses . . . and you? I don't know why you think that, but I can't picture it happening. Don't do something spur of the moment, Lilly. Talk to Ian, find out from him what is going on."

"You're right. Of course you are." She pushed the half-empty glass away and stood up. "I really need to get busy. I have to think. I have to go down to the house and see what I can salvage."

"And pack?"

"I didn't say that." She brushed past Jamie. "I'm sorry, I just don't know anymore. I thought I had everything planned out."

"You were in control."

Lilly dumped the tea in her glass into the sink and rinsed it out. "Okay, you win."

"I don't want to win." Jamie walked up behind her and gave her a loose hug. "Go to the house, do what you need to do, and I'll stay here with Shelby."

"Thank you, I would really appreciate that. Maybe I just need to get away by myself and think this through."

"Good idea. And when you come back, we'll have a cup of coffee. Decaf, of course."

Lilly hugged her friend. "You're a great friend, Jamie."

"Yeah, see that you don't forget that. And if you really love me, you'll bring some chocolate."

Lilly slipped her feet into her shoes. "You got it."

Chocolate would be good. Lilly could use some, too. Just like she could use some easy answers. Life seemed to be spinning out of control. In the last three months she had lost her sister, gained a child, moved, and gone through the nightmare of Carl. When would it all stop, or at least slow down?

She wanted her life back, the calm and organized existence she'd lived in Kansas City.

Ian cruised past his house when he saw that Lilly's van wasn't in the drive. She would be at her place, of course. She would want to clean it up and get it ready to move back into. Or she could be gone. He didn't want to think about that.

Her van wasn't parked in front of her house. It didn't look as if she had been there at all. Trash still littered the lawn. Clothing and dishes that Carl had tossed out of the broken windows were scattered all over the place. Nothing had been touched.

He had lost her again.

He jumped down from his truck and walked across the yard to the house. Carl had done a number on it, but nothing a few repairs wouldn't fix.

The storm that had blown through the other night had blown tree limbs all over the yard, adding more to the man-made damage. Ian picked up a few scattered tree limbs and carried them to an old burn pile behind the house.

He tried to push thoughts of Lilly from his mind. If she was gone, he couldn't do anything about it . . . unless he wanted to play caveman and drag her back to Oklahoma. He somehow doubted that would work.

He was nearly done when the sound of a car coming caught his attention. He turned and saw Lilly's van creeping down the road.

She wasn't gone. The world spun crazily, righting itself in his mind.

He dropped the last load of branches and dusted his hands off on his jeans before turning to walk back down the hill to where she had parked. Lilly stared at him from inside the van. For a long moment he wondered if she would get out. Or would she back out of the drive and leave him standing there alone?

Alone. He didn't want to be that word, not anymore. He had been content for the last few years. After spending these past weeks with Lilly and Shelby, he wasn't sure if he could be content anymore, not alone.

He wanted them in his life and he felt guilty praying for them to be a part of his world when maybe that wasn't God's will. He knew that Lilly was praying, too. What if she got a different answer?

She opened the van door and he backed up, giving her space to get out. She wouldn't look at him. His first warning that something was up.

"Lilly, I . . ." He choked on the words he had wanted to say and quickly substituted: "What are you doing here?"

"For a smart guy, it takes you awhile. This is my house, remember?" She smiled, a real smile. He noticed that her eyes no longer darted, looking for someone hiding around the corner. The guarded look was gone, too.

"I thought you left."

"I've been in town reserving a hotel."

"Why? You know that I have room."

"I can't stay with you." She looked around and he followed her searching gaze. "I obviously can't stay here. I know it seems a little dramatic, but I feel like a woman without a home."

She walked away from him, and he followed her across the dusty yard to the porch. She sat down on the front steps and he dropped down next to her.

"You're not leaving." He took the dandelion she had picked and rubbed it under her chin. She grinned, her smile brightening the world around her.

"You're having a hard time putting two and two together, aren't you?"

"Right now, I can't think past the fact that you're staying. I came here hoping to convince you to stay."

"I'm staying. The only thing I can't figure out is whether or not you're staying. I can't imagine this place without you."

"What?" Thoroughly confused, he shook his head, trying to connect the dots to a puzzle he didn't have all of the clues to. "Why do you think I wouldn't be here?"

A pink rush of color spread over her cheeks and up her nose. "The conversation with your dad about the job. I don't blame you for being interested. I guess I'm just surprised that you would leave what you have here."

He was lost without a map, and he wasn't about to ask for directions. Where in the world had she come up with the idea that he planned to leave Oklahoma? He rolled the question through his mind until he finally remembered.

"You heard my dad tell me about the job."

"Yes, and I heard you say you were interested."

"You didn't stay long enough to hear me say that it was a great opportunity for the right man, but I'm not the right man. Dad and I had the longest talk that night. We had a real conversation, one during which he actually listened, and for the first time understood that I have to make choices for myself, based on what I feel led to do."

"You're not leaving?" She bit down on her bottom lip, and tears welled up in her eyes. "I just thought you would want to be where your parents are and where life is easier."

"This is my home. I love my job here, and my horses. Dad has tried to push me for years. He's always wanted more for me than I've wanted for myself. Or so he thought."

"You're not leaving."

Hadn't she already said that? He was positive she had. And this time he wanted to make sure she had no doubts. He wanted to show her how he felt about her, and about leaving.

Lilly plucked another dandelion. She held it up to Ian's chin. "Do you love me?"

She brushed the flower under his chin, leaving a yellow streak behind. "Hmmm, do you think these flowers really tell the truth?"

Ian took hold of her hand. "I don't know about dandelions. I do know about my heart. And I love you, Lilly. I don't want you to leave. I don't know where I'd be without you."

"That's the thing, Ian. If I left, you'd be in the same place as when I came here. You'd still have your home, your practice and your friends."

"Okay, and for some reason that I don't understand, that's a bad thing and I'm in trouble?"

"No, not really. I realized something today. You see, I have a strong desire to be in charge of the chaos that is my life, and I realized today that change doesn't mean that life is out of control, because even in the middle of change, God is in control."

"Very wise. You're beautiful and intelligent." He touched the dandelion to her nose. "And I do love you. That's something I've known for a long time, and something I thought you could see. I love you enough to let you go. That isn't easy, but I can do it. And then I'm going to pray every day that God brings you back."

Lilly touched his cheek. Her fingers lingered on his jaw and slowly his face drifted closer to hers. Lilly closed her eyes, waiting, and hoping that this kiss was forever.

Ian's lips moved over hers, lingering on her mouth and drawing her heart closer to his. Lilly sighed and pulled away. It felt like a forever kiss.

"Where do we go from here?" She whispered the words as she leaned against his shoulder and his arms closed around her.

"I hope we go forward." Ian's hands moved across her back to her arms and he pulled her back. "Lilly, I know this has to be your decision, but I want you to know how I feel."

"I was hoping we would get to that sooner or later."

He laughed and bent to drop a kiss on her cheek. Lilly's fears faded and hope grew, hope for a future with a man who would always be there.

"I want you to stay, to give us a chance."

"I think I want that, too. I'm just afraid."

Ian reached for her hand, touched the top of her fingers and then lifted her hand to his lips. Lilly melted.

"Tell me what you're afraid of. If we're going to have a relationship, I want it built on honesty. I want to know what you're thinking. I want to know your fears. I want to work things out together."

"I'm afraid of losing who I am. I don't want to stop being strong."

"Have you ever looked at a lead rope?"

Lilly shook her head. "Ian, we're talking about our future, not horses."

He laughed, and holding her hand he stood up. "Come over to the truck. I want you to look at a lead rope."

Horses. Did they really have to talk horses in the middle of talking about their future? The answer was obviously yes.

At the truck, Ian let go of her hand. He reached into the box in the back of his truck and pulled out a red and white rope. He handed it to her.

"Okay, a lead rope. I'm happy for you."

He touched the corded threads. "It's a rope, but there are two cords, not one. Two, and they're twined together to make the rope stronger. Each cord is strong on its own, but when they're joined together, they're even stronger." He dropped the rope behind her and pulled her close to him. "Lilly, I want to make my life with you, not to take from you, but to join my life with yours."

Tears trickled from Lilly's eyes. She brushed them away, but more quickly took their place.

"I really hope that those are happy tears." He leaned toward her and kissed her cheeks, first one and then the other.

"Ian, if you're asking me to marry you, the answer is yes.

I want to marry you. I want to share my life with you."

"I was asking." He pulled her to him and held her close.

"I love you, Ian."

"I've wanted to hear that all of my life." He kissed her again, and this time Lilly felt as if her heart had taken wings and flown away.

ABOUT THE AUTHOR

BRENDA MINTON lives a chaotic, but wonderful, life in the Missouri Ozarks. She's a wife and home-schooling mother of three who poses as a sane adult on occasion. She's willing to speak to women's groups, if the women are willing to have her. Visit her Web site at www.BrendaMinton.com.